CW00382961

NIGEL'S INTRANET ADVENTURE

C.S. Rhymes

Copyright © 2020 C.S. Rhymes

All rights reserved

The characters and events portrayed in this book are fictitious. Any similarity to real persons, living or dead, is coincidental and not intended by the author.

No part of this book may be reproduced, or stored in a retrieval system, or transmitted in any form or by any means, electronic, mechanical, photocopying, recording, or otherwise, without express written permission of the publisher.

CONTENTS

Title Page

Copyright

Introducing Nigel   1

What's in a job title?   5

Dave, the comeback   8

Back home   13

Enroute to the Red Lion   17

Living it large in the Red Lion   21

The Morning After   29

The Mission Begins   36

Family catch up   43

Special Delivery   52

Assembly line   56

The Alpha Release   68

The No Show   73

Heads Up   80

The Reunion   83

The Big Boss   95

The Audit   98

The Aftermath   105

Fighting Back   107

The Demo   110

The Negotiation   118

INTRODUCING NIGEL

Nigel brought his mug close to his mouth, holding the mug in both hands. He didn't drink from it straight away, instead he shut his eyes and inhaled through his nose, breathing in the scent of his freshly made cup of coffee. He enjoyed the aroma for a short moment, before he tipped a mouthful of the warm, luxurious coffee into his mouth, savouring the different textures of the strong coffee mixed with the micro bubbles of hot frothy milk.

He opened his eyes and looked up from his cup of hot, steaming coffee to see his computer monitor on his desk. He could see the steam swirling as it rose from his mug in the reflection on his screen. He followed the steam upwards until he saw his own face reflected in the glass.

Nigel was in his mid-thirties, his hair starting to turn grey but the majority was still dark black. He wore silver framed glasses that were once fashionable, but he couldn't remember when that was, along with a matching silver Casio digital watch on his left wrist. Today, like most days in the office, he wore a pair of dark grey smart trousers with a well ironed white shirt with a red and blue striped tie.

Nigel worked in an office for a large sales company, his desk in the corner, out of the way of the busy hustle and bustle of the sales and marketing teams. The company he worked for was called

Amstaria, specialising in selling electronics, such as clock radios and USB dongles to retailers.

His official job title was 'Intranet Coordinator', but most people in the office didn't know what his job title was or what he actually did, just seeing him as the IT geek that sat in the corner. To be honest, Nigel didn't know what his job was either.

The cut throat world of Amstaria sales and marketing team had resulted in a continuous turnover of staff, with employees moving on to their next great opportunity, expanding their career and increasing their bonus. As a result, Nigel was the longest serving member of staff, seeming to everyone else as to have always been there. A part of the furniture.

The current sales manager (the one for that couple of months or so anyway) was walking around introducing a new member of staff to the rest of the office when he eventually got to Nigel.

"Ah hello there..." there was an unnecessary pause while the Sales Manager waited for Nigel to say his name.

"Nigel" prompted Nigel, wondering how long he could wait before it turned into a very awkward silence.

"Yes, of course, Nigel. Let me introduce you to Dave" he turned and gestured with an open palm towards the new starter "He has just started in the sales team and will be sitting next to Adam."

To Nigel, Dave looked like the run of the mill newby salesman, starting out with his first job from school, getting his first step on the career ladder. Dave was wearing a suit and tie, trying to impress on his first day at work, but this suit was quite ill fitting with sleeves too long and a belt tied tighter than was intended so it kept the suit trousers up. Dave's hair was slicked back, combed neatly, making the hair appear shorter than it actually was. It also looked to Nigel as if Dave was wearing a clip on tie.

Forcing his focus away from Dave's cheap suit and clip on tie, Nigel realised the sales manager was about to start talking again.

"So why don't you explain a bit about what you do here Nigel?" asked the Sales Manager as he really didn't know or even seem to want to know what Nigel did.

"Well, I work on the Intranet and..." starts Nigel.

"Right thanks for that." the sales manager interrupted. "No need to bore everyone with too much detail of computers and stuff like that. I'm sure you and Dave will be working together on some projects in the near future" the Sales Manager finished before walking back to his small office on the other side of the room.

Normally the new recruit would smile politely and also walk off following suit, but for some reason Dave was still there. "Did you say intranet?" asked Dave, "Don't you mean internet?"

Wow, an actual question from a new member of staff! This never happened. The question was even semi relevant and not just some stupid question about the weather over the weekend.

"Well, no. My job is looking after the company intranet." replied Nigel, "It's the internal website, so it's called an intranet."

"Ahh, I see" said Dave "That's cool. Maybe you could show me how it works sometime. I've got some product training with Adam starting in a minute but I'll come back over this afternoon if that's ok?"

"Sure, no problem" said Nigel "See you later."

And with that, Dave walked off to his meeting. Nigel thought to himself that that would be the last time he would ever speak to Dave. Occasionally people feel the need to be polite and start a conversation with Nigel at the coffee machine, but they are normally put off the idea of speaking to Nigel again after the word "Intranet" is pronounced.

Nigel thought there was something different about Dave, but he was unsure what it was? For some strange reason, the clip on tie and slicked back hair unsettled Nigel. "I must be imagining things" he thought to himself and carried on with his work. Well, I say work, but as no one really understood what the Intranet was, Nigel never really had any work to do.

WHAT'S IN A
JOB TITLE?

To be honest, Nigel didn't really do a lot at work. Well, he did a lot, just not much of what you could call work.

He had been working for the company longer than anyone else in the office, so no one that was there now knew who hired him and what his actual job was supposed to be.

Most of the time Nigel was left alone to his own devices, but every now and then you would hear random shouts from across the office such as "The printers got that flashy light thing again?" or "I dropped some water in the paper shredder and it made a funny noise".

Being the sole IT representative in the office, Nigel would walk over and ask politely "What's the problem?" and was answered with a shrug of the shoulders and the answer "I don't know, it was working fine earlier and it just stopped working..." with the expectation Nigel would get straight to it and fix whatever the problem was without any further information.

Nigel knew a bit about technology, being the Intranet Manager, but fixing flashing lights on printers and paper stuck in shredders was not his speciality. Nigel knew that most problems of an IT nature were solved by turning it off and on again, so he would try this and see what would happen. If that didn't do the trick, which actually worked surprisingly often, he just Googled the problem and would find a forum or YouTube video guide for how to fix it.

To the sales team's amazement it would normally fix the problem and the printer or shredder or whatever piece of office equipment it was would start working again. Not that any member of the sales team would ever say thank you to him, as he had just removed their excuse for not doing any work.

Anyway, in the time not spent rebooting office equipment, Nigel would spend his time reading on the internet. Nigel loved to read. It was one of the only reasons he was still "working" for Amstaria, with the other being the generous pay packet.

Nigel was not a fool. In fact he was exceptionally clever, he just let people think he was a bit simple to get an easy life. The benefit of being a long serving employee and having a new Sales Manager start every couple of months is the ability to persuade the new manager that the old one had agreed a new pay deal before he left, but didn't get round to finishing off the paperwork. The new manager, afraid of rocking the boat with the company's longest serving employee, would sign the paperwork and fax it off to HR.

Good pay and time to read were the perfect combination for Nigel, apart from the previously mentioned interruptions fixing the office equipment. The other great bonus to his office life was the great coffee machine he had managed to persuade one of the previous Sales Managers to install, at a significant cost which, ironically, ended up losing the Sales Manager his job for overspending. Nigel had explained to the Sales Manager how he had read a recent article on how great coffee could boost sales, omitting the fact that he found the article on the coffee machine manufacturer's blog page.

Nigel would read whatever he wanted to, not restricting his subject matter to any one subject. He would regularly start off by researching something he heard about on TV the night before, starting off with a bit of reading on Wikipedia, before moving on to news articles and blogs, followed by a bit more location research on Google Maps before moving onto the next interesting topic.

This kind of reading regularly sparked off many different offshoots to related subjects. The internet seemed to Nigel to be the fountain of all knowledge. Anything you wanted to know could be found online. Although Nigel could in theory get away with reading almost anything online, he took it upon himself to ensure he kept to a high moral standard. It seemed that somehow, no matter what subject he started off with, it would eventually lead to a "questionable" site.

Nigel had spent the morning finding out a bit more about Equatorial Guinea (today's random subject of choice), split up by regular coffee breaks, when he had a tap on the shoulder.

DAVE, THE COMEBACK

"**A**fternoon Nigel!" an unfamiliar voice spoke behind Nigel.

Nigel turned round to see who had interrupted him and was surprised to see the new employee, Dave, there with a cup of coffee in his outstretched hand, offering it to Nigel.

"Hi Nigel" said Dave "Latte Macchiato with no sugar, for you. Let's have a chat about the intranet. Meeting room one is free."

"Great, thanks, but how did you know about the coffee?" replied Nigel as they walked across the office to the meeting room. Dave didn't reply immediately, instead he waited for Nigel to sit down at the table in the meeting room and shut the door, before joining him. Dave made himself comfortable and took his time before starting to speak.

"I watched you earlier when you walked over to the coffee machine. Observation is one of my strong points. I can watch someone do something and then I seem to be able to copy it." added Dave, "I also observed the fact that you haven't actually done any work today, you seem to be visiting a load of websites about central Africa, Equatorial Guinea to be exact…"

"Ooh, well, umm" spat Nigel as he quickly finished a large mouthful of his Macchiato, trying not to choke on the hot liquid, "I was just doing a bit of research for a trip I'm planning"

"Is that right. I've actually done a bit more research into your browsing habits, looking at your browser history when you went and got your coffee this morning. It seems you do a lot of browsing. In fact, pretty much all day, every day..." Dave said smugly, looking at Nigel with a smirk on his face.

Nigel knew his secret was finally out. What was he going to do? He looked at Dave and saw the confidence in his eyes. He compared it to how he felt inside, a complete lack of self-belief after not even attempting anything, let alone actually achieving anything for so long. How could he compete with such an opponent as this?

He took a deep breath and filled his lungs in a vain attempt of fighting back.

"Please don't tell on me. I don't know if I could get another job. Why would anyone want to hire me?" as Nigel spoke his eyes looked down at the wooden table between them, not even brave enough to look his opponent in the eye, feeling his heart sink inside his chest.

He knew someday someone would find out that he didn't actually do any work, he just didn't expect it to be some newby on his first day at work. He thought by then he would have a plan. A way to get out of the situation, but any semblance of a plan had escaped from his mind.

"Ha ha ha ha!" chuckled Dave as his head went back, obviously enjoying the moment.

This was not the reaction Nigel had expected.

Nigel had played the scenario of being found out in his head many times before, but it never involved the other person in the scenario laughing. It had always ended with the other person standing over him shouting "Clear out your desk and don't come back!", followed by Nigel immediately obeying, walking over to his desk, standing there looking gormless for a few seconds before he realised he had no personal belongings at his desk and then running for the door as fast as he could before he started crying. Nigel would be so anxious to reach the outside that he would run down the stairs out of the office into reception before running head first into the large glass window, rather than the glass door next to the window. Visualising the impact of his bloodied nose splatter against the polished, clear glass panel was enough to shake him from his daydream and back into reality.

Dave was still completing his laugh, but now he was looking directly at Nigel with a friendly smile on his face and, strangely, his hand outstretched for a handshake.

"I don't understand... Aren't you going to tell the sales manager and get me fired?" stuttered Nigel.

"No Nigel, why would I do that?" smiled Dave. Nigel was perplexed. What was going on? Nigel could clearly say he had never met anyone like Dave before.

"I have a proposition for you, but before I asked you, I just couldn't help myself but see how you would react in a confrontation." said Dave. "I've only known you for a little while Nigel, but I know you can be so much more if you just believe in yourself a bit more. I think we can be great friends, you and I. Help each other out. What do you say?"

Nigel looked up from the table, realising that Dave's hand was outstretched for a handshake. Still not really comprehending what was going on he put his hand out and shook Dave's hand.

"Sorry about that Nigel, but I had a feeling that you were the person I was looking for the first time I met you." said Dave, "Shall I tell you what I saw in you Nigel?"

Not really sure what to say, not even sure he could say anything right now, Nigel just nodded slowly.

"Great!" said Dave, "I saw someone that was part of the furniture, but yet didn't really belong here. I saw someone that was stuck in a rut, just coming to work every day as they had nothing else to do, proving my theory after checking your browsing history."

It looked to Nigel like Dave was just getting started with his speech, but hearing Dave say these words drove home to him how pathetically true it was.

"I see someone that wants to get out of here and see the world." Dave continued "I see someone that wants to say they have truly lived. Not experienced life through a desktop monitor, reading about what other people have done and what they have experienced." He paused momentarily." You need to wake up Nigel."

It all started to make sense to Nigel now. Where had his dreams gone? Nigel looked down at the table, his mind erratically thinking. He would never ponder about why he was always reading about these places all over the world and all these different things on the internet, he just did. But hearing these words forced him to face the truth inside.

He hated his job; he hated coming to work every day. He wanted to achieve something with his life, he wanted to make a difference to the world, but that was all gone now.

The years of sitting at his desk, watching the people come and go through the revolving doors, no one utilising his skills and knowledge, realising that no one cared if he turned up for work or not. It had turned him into a mindless zombie. Days merging into weeks, into years, into a decade.

"Am I right?" asked Dave.

Nigel's eyes slowly rose from the table until they met Dave's eyes and there they stayed.

"Yes" replied Nigel.

"Good." Dave paused. "I think you are ready to hear my

proposition. Meet me in the Red Lion, in town at ten this evening." and with that Dave got up and left the meeting room.

Nigel felt his heart still racing in his chest. His emotions were all over the place. He couldn't face going back to his desk so he just sat there in the meeting room on his own while he tried to regain control. He sipped his coffee slowly, comforting and warming him from the inside, slowly regaining a sense of calm.

With his coffee now finished, he slowly walked back to his desk and sat down. Before he knew it, it was five o'clock and the clock in the office chimed five times, nudging Nigel from his stupor. He got up and walked out of the office.

BACK HOME

Nigel headed straight home from the office, putting his headphones on as he left the building and turning on some music, not really listening to it, just zoning out and ignoring all the people on the street as he walked. He lived in a small one bedroom apartment about two miles away from the office. It was a forty minute walk, which gave him more time to clear his head before he reached his front door.

Nigel didn't know what to think, what he did know was that he was feeling sick in his stomach. In a way he was excited about the unknown, but the feeling of safety with his dull, boring life was slipping away.

Nigel got his keys out of his pocket and fumbled with the lock, his hands shaking slightly, until he unlocked the door, pushed himself inside and slammed it firmly shut behind him. Normally he would just leave it at that but tonight he double locked the door and put the chain across to help him feel more secure, before moving to the living room and laying down in the middle of the floor.

A normal evening for Nigel involved sitting in his favourite old chair, watching TV, whilst browsing the net on his tablet, eating a microwave meal, before heading off to bed before 10pm.

Favourite old chair was one way of describing it. His only chair was another way of putting it.

Nigel lived alone so he didn't see the point in buying a two seater sofa. He was very careful with his money, but that didn't mean he never spent it. He carefully considered each purchase, reading reviews online to find the right product for him. Once he had made his choice, he then spent the next couple of days searching the web for the best price before placing his order.

Nigel wasn't rich. He was on a decent salary but he wanted the best for his investment. He did not do impulse buying. What he did buy would impress anyone. His favourite chair was a reclining, black leather armchair that he could sink into after a long day at work. What made this chair even better was the built-in back massager. The chair also had a pocket in the side for a tv remote. The remote in the pocket was not for any TV, it was for a 65" 4K Ultra HD High Dynamic Range curved OLED screen, along with the matching cinema quality surround sound system and 4K blu ray player.

Nigel's apartment could be described as quite pokey, but looked great with the minimal furniture making the most of the available space. The kitchen only contained a handful of kitchen units with a distinct lack of worktop space, but Nigel didn't really cook. He ate microwave meals, but not low price frozen meals, they were high end supermarket ready meals, both low in fat and salt, nutritious and tasty. Alongside the microwave oven on the worktop was a shining, silver, professional coffee making machine, filled with high quality fresh coffee beans that are ground as needed.

Nigel's bathroom, although it didn't actually contain a bath, contained more tech, with a high pressure massaging shower in one corner and smart scales in the other that measured your weight and body fat and transmitted it to his phone via Bluetooth. Not that Nigel had to worry about his weight, he just found the statistics interesting.

The bedroom was the only room that didn't contain any technology. Nigel had once read that too much artificial light in the bedroom could affect your sleep patterns so he ensured this room was free of tech. Another, more realistic, reason for the lack of furniture was that once the double bed and wardrobe were in the room, you couldn't actually fit anything else in the room if you wanted to.

Nigel, still laying down on the floor of his living room, remembered that he was supposed to meet Dave at the Red Lion in town in just a few hours.

Taking a deep breath, he composed himself before standing up, quickly realising he had stood up a bit too quickly, getting a head rush, causing him to lie back down again as he was before, waiting for the feeling to stop.

This time he got up slowly and sat in his armchair and turned the TV on, trying to regain a sense of normality. The huge, curved TV blinked into life, along with the surround sound. The TV was set to an old movie channel from the night before and was playing "The Godfather".

"I'm going to make him an offer he can't refuse" blasted out from the surround sound. Nigel quickly reached for the remote and turned the TV back off.

Nigel started thinking back to what Dave had said to him at the end of their meeting earlier. What kind of proposition could Dave have for Nigel? How could he fit into his plans, whatever they were?

Nigel was slowly starting to feel more intrigued, than scared. He was actually looking forward to finding out what Dave wanted. He thought about his normal evening of watching tv and reading from the internet and, much like his work life, he realised just how boring he had become.

"Right, I'm going to the Red Lion!" Nigel said to himself. He realised he didn't actually know where the Red Lion was, in fact, he couldn't remember the last time he went to any pub? What was he going to wear?

He went into his bedroom and opened the wardrobe and stared at the row of black office trousers and white shirts. No good. Then he remembered an old pair of jeans he had put in a drawer for safe keeping. Nigel pulled open the drawer and removed the jeans and hoped they still fit. He removed his tie and left his shirt on, thinking smart casual would be the way to go.

Now all he had to do was find his way to the pub.

ENROUTE TO THE RED LION

Many people use their phones as a sat nav in their car, but not many, if any, use it whilst walking. The main reason for this is because you look like a complete idiot walking along with your phone out in front of you looking at a map. This was exactly what Nigel was doing, whilst wearing his work shirt, old jeans and work shoes, walking down the High Street, enroute to the Red Lion.

The town he lived in had changed quite a lot since he had last visited. He didn't have much, if any, need of visiting the High Street anymore. He ordered everything online and assumed that everyone did the same these days. He was surprised to see so many people about in town this late at night, with many of the large department stores still open.

As well as shoppers, there were also a lot of people out for a drink. This surprised Nigel even more. People drinking on a Monday night. Didn't people have jobs to go to in the morning?

Nigel stopped off at a newsagent as he needed some cash for the pub, putting his phone in his pocket. He had no need for carrying cash these days, with online shopping and contactless payments, cash was a relic of a bygone age, unless that is, you were off to the pub for a pint. He walked over to the counter to speak to the shop assistant.

"Hi there, I was wondering if you did cashback" said Nigel.

"Yeah sure, what you buying?" said the shop assistant

"Oh, um, some chewing gum and twenty pound cash back please" replied Nigel

"Do a U-Turn where possible" shouted Nigel's phone in a dodgy American synthesised voice. "Find a road. Signal lost, Signal lost, Signal Lost" it continued.

"What the hell is that?" said the assistant

Nigel had forgotten to turn his sat nav off before coming into the shop. He quickly removed his phone from his pocket to turn the sound off, embarrassed by the constant "Signal Lost" announcement continuously being blurted out. Nigel had his wallet in his hands already and was trying to flip the silence switch on the side of his phone at the same time.

"Signal Lost, do a U-turn when possible" it continued. Nigel flicked the switch to finally silence the phone but was a bit too vigorous, causing the phone to slip out of his hands and start to fall to the floor. It was as if the phone was falling in slow motion to Nigel looking down at it. The phone rotated around in a smooth arc, the screen facing downwards, then upwards, then down again, before finally hitting the floor screen side down.

A loud crunching sound followed as cracks spread from one corner of the screen across the device. The screen transformed instantly from a shiny single piece of glass, to countless tiny pieces of jagged glass.

"Ha ha ha" laughed the shop assistant. "You didn't want to do that!"

Nigel bent down and picked up his shattered phone, thinking how could this day get any worse, when suddenly the seam in his old jeans made a horrible ripping sound. That's how it could get worse, sparking even louder laughter from the shop assistant.

Nigel stood up and paid for the chewing gum, getting his cash back, without saying a word and avoiding making eye contact with the shop assistant, quickly left the shop.

Nigel remembered the department stores were still open so he quickly walked into the nearest one he could find to look for a new pair of trousers. As he entered, he realised the shop was closing soon. He ran to the menswear department looking for another pair of jeans. He found a pair of black jeans in his size, grabbed them off the shelf and ran to the till to pay before the shop shut for the night.

Feeling a bit more composed he left the shop and looked for a place to change. The street lights weren't working here, probably in an effort to save money on the council's electric bill. As he was walking along the High Street a voice shouted his name.

"Nigel, over here mate!"

Nigel turned to see Dave waving at him from the entrance to the Red Lion. Not wanting to go into the pub with a ripped pair of trousers, Nigel wanted to make his excuses and go home. Things were not going his way and he saw the previous events as a sign that this was not a good thing to be doing. Luckily, Dave couldn't see the ripped trousers due to the lack of street lighting, so at least he didn't have to explain that to him.

"Oh, hi Dave, umm, I'm afraid that I can't come into the pub, I've got to get home" said Nigel.

"Nonsense, you're here now. I've got a table near the back." encouraged Dave "Quick, let's go in before we lose it." Dave put his arm around Nigel's shoulders and shepherded him through the door of the pub.

Nigel was panicking now, unsure what to do, he looked around the interior of the pub and saw the sign for the gents on the left of the pub entrance.

"I've just got to visit the gents then I'll be right with you." lied Nigel.

"Ok, that's cool." said Dave, "Mine's a pint of lager, see you in a min"

Nigel hurried into the gents and found a cubicle so he could quickly change trousers and restore some of his dignity. This however, did not go to plan.

Nigel removed the trousers from the bag and gasped. Somehow, in the rush in the store, he hadn't realised he had purchased skin tight leather trousers.

LIVING IT LARGE IN
THE RED LION

Nigel had removed his ripped jeans and was attempting to put his newly purchased leather trousers on, as discretely as possible in the tiny cubicle in the toilet. He had removed his shoes, but was standing on top of them to avoid standing on the wet floor, whilst he struggled to pull up the trousers. He told himself it was just water, but was struggling to convince himself it was true due to the awful smell that permeated the air.

He managed to pull the trousers all the way up and fastened the zip and button. Nigel let out a gasp of relief, only to lose his carefully placed balance on his shoes, with one of his feet slipping off the shoe completely and onto the sopping wet floor, soaking the bottom of his sock.

Nigel hurriedly lifted his foot off the floor and put his dripping foot back into his shoe, followed by the other shoe. He unlocked the cubicle and stepped out into the gents and then on towards the bar. As he walked his leather trousers made a strange squeaking noise with every step, followed by a squelching noise every other step from his wet shoe. Nigel opened the door and breathed another sigh of relief as he heard the loud music coming from a band in the far corner of the pub that would drown out the awkward noise of his walking.

"What did he want to drink again?" Nigel thought to himself as he walked towards the bar. "Oh yeah, a lager."

"What can I get you mate?" asked the barmaid, stirring Nigel from his thoughts.

"A lager for my friend and I'll have a…" Nigel paused. Nigel hadn't been out for years. He had no idea what to order for himself. "Make it two lagers" he finished. If you can't beat them, join them.

"So three pints then?" replied the barmaid.

"Umm sure" replied Nigel nervously without really thinking about it. Nigel had meant two pints in total, but the barmaid had obviously thought he wanted two pints for himself. For some reason he didn't want to contradict the lovely, if a bit dim, barmaid. Maybe it was her smile, maybe it was her eyes, maybe it was her 'other assets'. Anyway, he justified it to himself by thinking he was playing catch up with Dave who probably had a couple of pints by now anyway.

Nigel paid the lovely barmaid with a ten pound note, expecting change, but getting none in return. Prices had obviously gone up since the last time he had been out. He picked up the three pints, balancing them in the standard triangle formation. That brought back memories of his old pub crawls with his mates, carrying pints across a crowded pub to the table where his mates would be sitting, except today he was walking towards a table where a bloke named Dave was sitting, who he had only met for the first time today.

"Excellent Nigel, you read my mind." said Dave over the noise of the band. The band looked like students, very old students that is. They looked like a band that had been playing together for years, playing the same songs each week, waiting to hit the big time, but ended up playing in the same group of pubs over and over again. They weren't bad, they were just a bit average.

Nigel carefully lowered the three pints onto the table in front of him and sat down next to Dave. Nigel went to move one of the pints over towards Dave, until he realised that Dave already had two full pints in front of him.

"I was wondering what was keeping you and I was gasping for a drink, so I thought I'd get a couple in whilst I was waiting for you" explained Dave. "I've been known to get a couple at a time, but three, that's dedication!"

"Oh, I bought one of these for you" replied Nigel.

"Ha ha, you don't have to play it down for me. I'm sorted, you have them. Can't show up hung over tomorrow at work. It's only my second day, after all." joked Dave.

"Cool, thanks" said Nigel. It had been a while since Nigel had been drinking, now he faced the prospect of having to finish off three pints, with less than an hour until closing time. "Better get started" thought Nigel as he picked up the first drink and started sipping. At least Dave hadn't mentioned the leather trousers.

"So, do you come here often?" asked Nigel, trying to make small talk.

"Easy tiger!" laughed Dave. "I'm not that kind of guy!"

Dave seemed completely unphased by the comment, just sitting there chilled, sipping, or more accurately, gulping down his first pint. Nigel on the other hand was horrified with himself, almost choking on a mouthful of beer.

"No, umm, I didn't mean it like that. I just wondered if this was your local?" Nigel spurted.

"I know, I was just winding you up. Which is far too easy by the way." said Dave, "You need to chill out a bit and try and have a good time. Enjoy life!"

Twice in one day Dave had hit the nail on the head. Nigel was starting to like Dave. He was obviously going to be a disruptive force in his life, but maybe that was what he needed.

"Yeah, this is my local pub. It's not really that local for me, more like a half hour walk." said Dave. "It's not for the beer or the atmosphere and definitely not this crap band that seem to be playing here every couple of weeks. It's for the view", Dave pointed subtly over to the barmaid, who was vigorously polishing one of the beer pumps.

"She's nice" said Nigel, "What's her name?"

"Tracey" said Dave. "I was going to ask her out once, but the landlord interrupted our conversation and told her to change the barrel."

"Oh, so why haven't you asked her out since?" asked Nigel.

"Well, the timing has never seemed right since. You know the feeling you may have missed your opportunity, when everything seemed to be lined up, but it wasn't meant to be." replied Dave, as he moved his eyes away from Tracey and looked down into his half empty pint glass before taking another gulp.

"Anyway" said Dave, "Tonight is not supposed to be about missed opportunities, it is all about new opportunities. I bet you are wondering why I asked you to meet me here and what I've got planned?"

"Well, yes, it had crossed my mind" said Nigel.

"Ok, here goes" said Dave, his face turning into a wide grin. "I need you Nigel. I need your insider knowledge and your access at Amstaria, because I have an idea. I have an idea that will change the face of human experience forever."

Oh dear, thought Nigel. He may have worked for Amstaria for a long time, but in terms of insider knowledge of the company, that was pretty much non-existent. Nigel's saving grace was his access to the computer systems. As Intranet manager, he had access to a wide range of different computer systems, not that he ever had reason to use any of them in his non-existent job.

"What I need from you Nigel, is for you to get me access to some very specific parts that Amstaria sell." continued Dave. "I need you to use your computer skills and access to divert these parts from their normal destinations and send them to our office so I can make my plan work."

Nigel was feeling a bit apprehensive about Dave's plan. He could probably figure out how to get some parts sent over for samples easy enough, if he could remember where he left the instruction manual he printed out all those years ago, but what did he want the parts for?

A thought suddenly jumped into Nigel's mind. Maybe he was a new age terrorist, Macgyvering some deadly Weapon of Mass Distraction out of spare parts to stick it to the man, just because he could. But then Dave seemed far too chilled out for that, if the few hours that Nigel had known him for were anything to go by.

Nigel's confidence wasn't at its highest point right now, but it was aided by the first pint of beer working its way through his system. "You're not making a bomb or something are you?" blurted Nigel.

Nigel wished he hadn't said that, particularly not quite so loud, and particularly at the exact same moment the band finished their song when the room went silent. The few people in the pub, including the band, turned and looked at Nigel and Dave.

Dave, however, was his usual laid back self. "Ha ha, good one mate!" he replied in a suitably loud voice so the rest of the room could hear, "The band are pretty crap, but that's a bit of an extreme solution."

Before Nigel could answer he heard a reply coming back from the band's PA system. "Thanks for your support, YOU BASTARDS!", before they continued playing their next song.

"Like I said Nigel, you need to chill out." continued Dave, "My cause is more long term than blowing myself or other things up and definitely more worthy. It's something called money!"

Nigel didn't know what to say, so he took a rather large swig of beer, finishing his second pint and moving on to the third, waiting for Nigel to continue.

"Have you heard of virtual reality?" Dave asked.

"Yeah, I've read a lot about it online. There are lots of headset manufacturers trying to make the best experience possible with the best games. It's predicted to be a billion pound market in a few years." Nigel was glad he had some knowledge of something in the conversation for once.

"But what does a few spare parts from Amstaria have to do with Virtual Reality?"

"This is the cleverest part of my plan. We take a few different products and combine them together to make our own headset, but the biggest problem with Virtual Reality is the software, not the hardware."

So Nigel now understood Dave's was motivated by money, but he didn't see how this plan was going to work if massive corporations were still struggling to make it work with massive budgets.

"I'll be honest, this actually sounds quite an interesting hobby, but what are you going to do about the software?" asked Nigel.

"Hobby? Think bigger Nigel, think worldwide, think global domination!" Dave smiled at Nigel before picking up his pint glass and taking a large mouthful of beer. "One step at a time Nigel, you get the parts sorted and I'll sort the software. So are you in?"

"Well, what's the deal then?" asked Nigel

"Of course, of course, I forgot that part." replied Dave, "Let's split everything 50 - 50 between me and you. I propose that we both put a quid in to this company right now and make it official."

Nigel would normally want to go away, think about it and research it online for a few days before making a decision. Maybe it was the way Dave sold it, maybe it was the sense of adventure, or maybe it was just the two and a half pints he had drank. What he did know was that he was fed up with his day to day life. He felt like he had been awoken by the events of today and wanted it to continue tomorrow.

"I'm in" said Nigel, before putting his hand out for Dave to shake. They shook hands and then toasted with their half empty pint glasses before downing the remaining beer.

"Great! I knew you would be!" said Dave, "I'll give you a list of parts tomorrow morning and we can go from there."

"Great, see you tomorrow" replied Nigel, who then got up to leave, feeling full of energy.

Two things happened at the same time. The first was Nigel suddenly felt the effect of the three pints hit him all over, from his feet, to his balance in his inner ear. The second was a loud squeaking noise as his leather trousers rubbed together. This made Nigel massively self-conscious, but rather than just accepting it and carrying on walking in a drunk like manner, he tried very hard to do the opposite and overcorrected his drunken stature falling completely over, face first onto the floor.

Nigel blinked a few times and got his bearings for a few seconds before realising there was a hand stretched out ready to help him up. Dave helped Nigel to his feet and was laughing again.

"Ha ha ha, I take it the beer has gone straight to your head! Definitely time to call it a night." said Dave.

"Yep. I'm going to have to agree with you there Dave" replied Nigel.

Nigel shook his head from side to side to try and clear his head, but unfortunately this resulted in his vision spinning more than before. After the room stopped spinning he noticed the barmaid looking over at them.

"So are you going to try your luck with the barmaid again tonight then Dave?" Nigel asked.

"Nah, not tonight. Not after the display you just put on" joked Dave, "and anyway, I think she is rather taken by you in those leather trousers!"

Nigel at this point would normally go all red and embarrassed and start mumbling, but instead he felt strangely confident.

"Well, there's a funny story about these trousers..." smiled Nigel "maybe I can tell you all about it at our next meeting".

"See Nigel, you're chilling out already. Discovering that long lost sense of humour." said Dave.

"Right, time to go. See you tomorrow!" replied Nigel, and with that they walked out the pub, past the smiling barmaid, who turned to watch them as they left. The two new friends smiled and nodded at each other before they turned away from each other and made their way to their respective homes, with Nigel's new trousers continuing their squeaking noise all the way.

THE MORNING AFTER

The next morning, Nigel woke up with a start as his alarm started ringing. He reached over to his bedside table to turn it off, but somehow overstretched and fell out of the bed. He quickly reached back up to the bedside table and turned the alarm off. Strangely, Nigel still heard a ringing noise in his ears and he had a thumping headache to match.

Nigel staggered to the bathroom and turned on the shower. He stood under the warm running water for a few minutes, trying to make himself feel more human again and hoping the water running over his head would soothe his headache.

Nigel dried off and got himself dressed. He went downstairs and used his state of the art coffee machine to make himself his usual coffee, but today he pressed the button to make the coffee contain a double espresso instead of a single. He picked up his coffee and walked into his living room and went to sit down in his favourite chair. As he bent down he suddenly felt a twinge from around his groin area.

"Those bloody leather trousers, chafing!" he thought to himself.

He sat down and tried to make himself as comfortable as he could and slowly sipped his coffee, finally starting to feel better, and ran through the events from the previous evening. Any way he put it, he had made a complete arse of himself, but at least he had a good time. Dave was having a definite effect on Nigel's life and he was unsure where it was going, but he was excited to find out.

Nigel checked his watch and realised it was time to get going for work. He finished his coffee, feeling the strength of the double espresso at the bottom of the cup, and walked to the door. He put on his jacket and then his shoes, before he remembered his shoes were still soggy on the inside. He removed his shoes and socks and ran upstairs to get a new pair of socks and a new pair of shoes from his wardrobe, before putting them on and starting his regular walk to work.

Normally he would walk to work in silence, head down, but today Nigel was looking all about, taking in his surroundings as if he had never walked that route before. He walked along the road listening to the sound of the trees moving in the wind, admiring the architecture of the buildings and watching the people rushing around, making their way to work.

It brought back memories of when Nigel left university and got his first proper job and made his first walk to walk all those years ago. Back then he was full of confidence, eager to make use of his newly earned degree. He was looking forward to the challenge of work, the learning curve and getting up to speed. He had dreams of where his career might go and what success he might achieve.

On his first day he walked through the door and spoke to the receptionist.

"Good morning, how are you?" asked Nigel.

"Yes..." replied the receptionist, looking unimpressed.

"My name's Nigel, I'm here to see Mr Vaughn. It's my first day today." replied Nigel, enthusiastically.

"Mr Vaughn?" said the receptionist, looking blankly at him, "Oh, you mean Richard. Richard Vaughn?"

"Yes, that's him. He gave me my interview last month and told me to ask for him when I started. He said he would give me the tour and the induction personally." replied Nigel.

"Yeah, Richard left a couple of weeks ago. Got a new job on the other side of town." said the receptionist.

"Oh, okay, so do you know who I need to speak to?" Nigel questioned.

"Well, no one really. They haven't replaced him." the receptionist looked puzzled and then finished with, "Take a seat and I'll make some calls. You might want to get yourself a coffee."

With that, the receptionist picked up the phone and started talking, but looked like she didn't get the reply she wanted, before hanging up and redialling. This continued over and over for the next ten minutes. After five of the ten minutes, Nigel went and sat down, not sure what to do with himself. This was not the start to his career he had dreamed of.

Five minutes later, the receptionist called out to him.

"Hi Nathan, I just spoke to someone from sales who said they will send someone down to collect you shortly."

Not sure if she was speaking to him, Nigel looked around, noticing he was the only one there, he assumed she just got his name wrong and she was speaking to him. Maybe this was just a little speed bump on the start of his journey. He got up and helped himself to a coffee while he waited to be collected. It turned out to be a good thing for Nigel to get a coffee, as the short wait he was promised turned out to be a not so short thirty minutes.

A man walked down the stairs at the other end of the reception from where Nigel was sitting. He walked over to the receptionist and started talking to her. After about a minute, he turned to look over his shoulder at Nigel, staring for a few seconds, before continuing his conversation with the receptionist.

The man finished talking and started walking over to Nigel. "Hello there, I'm Simon, the head of Sales here at Amstaria." he said, extending his hand out towards Nigel.

"Hello Simon, I'm Nigel" replied Nigel tentatively, standing up and shaking Simons hand.

"Nice to meet you Nigel." began Simon. "I'm afraid that there has been a bit of a mix up with your paperwork. It seems Richard didn't complete the new starters process before he left. We didn't know you were coming today."

"Oh... Umm" said Nigel, trying to think of a witty and confident reply. Luckily Simon carried on before the silence got too awkward.

"It's not a problem. Let me show you where you will be sitting and I'll give you a quick tour round the office."

"That sounds great." Nigel smiled, relieved to hear that his job still existed.

Nigel followed Simon to the other end of reception and up the stairs, noticing Simon and the receptionist make eye contact for a little bit too long. Something going on between these two obviously, Nigel thought to himself.

At the top of the stairs was a set of double doors leading to the office. Simon got there first and held the door open for Nigel. As Nigel walked in he could see a large open plan office with four banks of desks in the middle of the office and a couple of desks at the far side of the office separated from the rest. There were also a couple of small offices next to the staff kitchen. Each of the banks of four desks sat up to eight people. There were a few people talking on phones, mingled with the sound of keyboard keys clicking.

Simon walked into the office and started speaking to everyone. The sound of clicking halted immediately.

"Good morning everyone." Simon started, "We have a new started here today called Nigel. He was supposed to be working for Richard, but as Richard no longer works here Nigel will be doing Richards old job."

"Morning, hello, alright" murmured the crowd politely, before turning back to their screens and recommencing making the clicking sounds again.

Nigel wondered what it was that Richard used to do and what his new job actually was, but it didn't seem like the right time to ask that question. He didn't want to make a bad impression to the head of sales on his first day.

Simon showed Nigel where the fire exits were, where the toilets were and where the staff kitchen was. Nigel noted the coffee machine on the worktop. It looked like a good machine, but it could do with a bit of a clean before he would use it.

"Let me show you your desk." Simon said as he started walking past the banks of desks and over to the couple of desks on their own. One of the desks was piled high with half open cardboard boxes and packaging materials. The other desk had a computer screen, keyboard and mouse, but was also covered in various pieces of paper and a layer of dust.

"This is your desk" Simon said, pointing to the desk with the computer and mountain of paper on it. "Your first job is to sort your desk out and then I'll send you an email with some more work later in the day."

"Great" said Nigel, trying to sound enthusiastic about his newly assigned task.

"That's what I like to hear Nigel. We need more enthusiastic people like you in this place. I think you will settle in well here." with that, Simon walked off and headed towards one of the small offices.

Nigel sat down at the desk and started trying to sort the various pieces of paper into piles, not that he could work out any logic of how the paper should be organised. Once the paper was out of the way he looked for a way to remove the dust. He spotted the stationary cupboard nearby and walked over to it. Nigel opened the cupboard and found it sparsely populated, with a single pack of pens and a notepad. Nigel grabbed a pen and the notepad in case he might need it and returned to his desk. He decided to use one of the old pieces of paper as an improvised duster and started to clear the dust of the desk.

It wasn't a particularly amazing effort of cleaning the desk, but he thought it would do for now, especially with the lack of supplies. Nigel sat down in his chair again and took stock of his newly acquired workstation. He moved the mouse and the screen flickered to life. The computer was already booted to Windows and ready to use. No need to log in.

He clicked the email icon and the email client opened and started to populate with emails. This seemed to take a very long time, with some emails from five years previous. The emails were addressed to Richard Vaughn. It seems that Richard Vaughn had never opened his email in his entire history of working for the company.

Just then, an email came into the inbox that caught Nigel's attention. The email subject was "New master password for the server". Nigel's curiosity got the better of him and he clicked the email to read it. It was from IT helpdesk and contained the master username and password, along with instructions to log in to the main company server. He flagged the email as he thought it might be useful later.

Nigel then sat and waited for Simon to send him an email or to come back over and give him some work to do. Nigel didn't want to make a fuss on his first day. He wanted to make a good impression, so he decided to try and make himself look busy. He found an instruction manual called 'Amstaria Intranet Management 'in one of the drawers in the desk, opened the cover and started reading.

Once he had read the book from cover to cover, he checked his emails. Still no messages. He decided to find something else to read and remembered a blog post he had started reading the previous night, so he looked around the office, but no one was paying him any attention, so he opened up the browser on the computer and typed the blog address in and started reading.

Nigel never did get that email from Simon. He just kept reading.

Nigel was brought back to reality by the loud sound of a bus horn beeping at him. He was waiting at the traffic lights, about to cross, but the bus decided it didn't want to wait for pedestrians today and ran the red light, narrowly missing Nigel's toes.

Rather than making Nigel feel scared, it made him feel alive. He enjoyed the thrill.

After the bus had passed, he crossed the road and entered the door into that same reception as all those years ago. Nothing had changed, apart from the receptionist, where there seemed to be a different one each week.

THE MISSION BEGINS

Nigel walked up the stairs to the office and walked over to his desk at the far side. First things first, he turned his computer on and then went to the kitchen and made himself a coffee. He stood sipping the hot coffee in the kitchen and looked out across the office. He looked at the faces of the various employees and tried to put names to the faces, but he soon realised he didn't know any of them. The only employee he did know was the one that started the previous day, but he was not yet at his desk.

Nigel wondered if Dave was also feeling a bit worse for ware after the drinks last night, but at that moment Dave walked confidently through the door, again wearing his ill fitting suit and slicked back hair, and walked to his desk and sat down. Nigel was glad to see him but Dave didn't even look at him.

A bit confused, Nigel walked back to his desk, sat down and looked at his computer screen. But rather than doing what he would do any other day and opening up Wikipedia and reading, he searched his email for anything mentioning the company intranet. Nigel thought it was about time he got to learn what his job was supposed to be. Otherwise, how was he going to order those parts for Dave's plan?

After 10 minutes he realised that email won't help him, as he was the only one that would have sent emails about the intranet, but as he never used the intranet, let alone email people about it there would be little point looking.

Instead, Nigel opened the bottom drawer of his desk and pulled out the dusty old manual that he read on his first day. He blew the dust off the cover, but due to his close proximity to the wall, the dust blew back into his face causing him to cough out loud. Once his coughing fit had passed he looked behind him and realised that everyone was looking at him.

"Just catching up on some reading" said Nigel smiling, "Every day is a school day"

Everyone made various tutting noises and carried on with their work, or at least making the loud clicking noises from their keyboards and pretending to work. Nigel wondered how many other staff were doing the same as him and sitting at their desk wasting their time, waiting for the day to end.

Or at least, what he used to do. Now he had a mission.

Nigel started reading the manual and the first page gave him the first clue he needed. The intranet was a site called Amstaria Portal, so he typed that into his browser and pressed enter.

The progress bar started to move across the screen, but at an exceptionally slow rate. The bar got about half way and waited there for a bit, before deciding, nope, I don't know what to do and returned a 404 page not found message. A similar feeling was coming from Nigel. Well that's not a great start, he thought to himself.

Nigel decided that the best course of action was to keep reading the manual. There had to be an answer in there somewhere. He turned to the next page in the manual and then he started to remember this section of the manual. It was about installing and configuring the server for the intranet. He had skipped past this the first time thinking it of little use, but thought he might as well read it this time. After all, there may be some troubleshooting advice.

There was the standard health and safety information that all manuals contained but no one ever read. They contained useful tips like don't use the hair dryer in the bath and don't iron clothes whilst wearing them.

The second paragraph was about installing the server in your office and a nice diagram of where to plug each port. You know the type of diagram that says plug the USB cable into the USB port and the HDMI cable into the HDMI port. Nigel suddenly realised that he hadn't ever seen a server in the office. Maybe it needed rebooting or something?

Nigel started looking around his desk for a computer that looked like the one in the picture, with the Amstaria logo on the front of it. There was nothing on his desk, so he decided to look under the desk. He was crawling around under the desk before he felt a presence behind him. Nigel turned round slowly and saw a pair of highly polished shoes, leading up to a crisp suit, finally followed by the face of the head of sales.

"What are you doing?" said the head of sales in an inquisitive voice (again, Nigel not remembering his name, so Nigel thought I'll call him shiny shoes from now on).

"I, uh, dropped a pencil" lied Nigel.

"What, you mean the one on your desk?" said shiny shoes, sarcastically.

"Oh, there it is. Thank you"

"Hmmm. I'll never understand you IT people" finished shiny shoes, before turning and walking over to someone else to start moaning at them for nothing in particular.

Nigel tucked his shirt back in from his adventure under the desk and sat back in his office chair. He straightened his back and sat up straight, sure that shiny shoes was still watching him.

Nigel had a slightly different perspective from this straight up position than from his usual slouching, reading position. He could now look onto the other desk near his and saw the boxes that had been there since he had started. When Nigel had started he assumed that the boxes had been emptied and just dumped there, but when he looked at the box again, he could see the Amstaria logo on the front of the box and a picture of a computer that was very similar to the diagram on the intranet manual.

Nigel stood up, as professionally as possible (in case shiny shoes was still watching), walked to the other desk and opened the box.

There, below some packing beads, was the intranet server!

No wonder the intranet didn't work. The server had never been plugged in, let alone needing rebooting!

Nigel took the server out of the box and stood it on the desk. He fished around in the box and pulled out a bag of leads. Nigel hastily plugged in the cables into their relevant ports and plugged the other ends into the sockets on the desk. He then pressed the big power button in the middle of the front panel.

A little light flashed on, then off, then on, quickly followed by one more light, then a third light. The server made a quiet whirring noise.

Nigel seemed satisfied it was working and then went back and sat down at his desk. He quickly clicked the refresh button on his browser and the progress bar started moving slowly across the screen again. The bar got halfway across again, but this time it continued moving and got to 100%. The page had loaded and Nigel was finally logged on to the intranet!

This had been his most productive day ever and it wasn't even 10am yet!

Nigel's email pinged an alert. It was a meeting request from Dave, with the subject "Intranet training". The meeting was scheduled for 10:30, so Nigel carried on with the instructions for setting up the server and logging on ready to go.

The meeting reminder pinged again, only five minutes to go. Nigel was happy with the progress he was making. He had logged on to the server and started to get things connected. The server was now downloading loads of updates, updates that should have been downloaded over the years since the server was first delivered.

Nigel left the server downloading and went to the meeting room and waited for Dave. Dave walked in soon after, carrying a notepad. Nigel had just about got over the alcohol from the previous night but Dave looked as fresh as if he had 20 hours sleep. He was obviously used to a beer or two.

"Mornin 'Nigel" said Dave. "How you feeling today? No leather trousers today I see"
"Well, I didn't want to make a habit out of it" replied Dave, "I might start enjoying wearing them"

"Nice. Nice" laughed Dave. "Anyway, let's get to business as I need to spend some more time catching up on the sales information pack I was given yesterday. I just wanted to read it over a few more times to make sure I know it all."

"Ok, great." said Nigel, impressed with Dave's commitment to his new job. "What do you need from me?"

"Right then Nigel, I have written out a list for you as promised. I was in a bit of a rush writing it so I apologize for the writing." Nigel said as he tore a page out of his notepad and handed it to Nigel.

Nigel glanced at the list and started trying to read it. The writing was a bit difficult to read, going from one line to another and a shaky handwriting style.

"Did you write this on the bus or something?" joked Nigel to Dave.

"Yeah, something like that" said Dave, sounding less confident than usual, but followed it up in his usual confident manner with "Well, I didn't want to make it too easy for you!"

"Yeah, cool." replied Nigel. "I'll see what I can do. When did you need it all by?"

"The end of the week would be great" said Dave. "Thanks for your help. I better go back to work. Those sales packs won't read themselves" joked Dave as he go up and headed back to his desk.

Nigel had the room booked for another twenty minutes so he thought he would spend the time re-writing the list into a more coherent fashion so he had an easy to read list once he was ready with the server to order the parts. Nigel finished writing the part numbers down from Dave's list without really knowing what any of them were, let alone how they would come together to make Virtual Reality equipment.

Nigel turned the piece of paper over, ready to fold it up and put it in his pocket, but then he noticed a sketch on the back. He turned it upside down and back to front in his hands a few times before it started to make sense to him what it was. Dave had drawn a sketch of a person wearing some kind of mask and gloves, but the person was lying down rather than standing or sitting up.

Knock, knock, knock.

Someone was knocking on the door. Nigel quickly folded the piece of paper into his pocket and covered up his own list, just before the door opened.

"Oh, hello again." it was shiny shoes again. Nigel had managed not to speak to him for weeks at a time and now he couldn't get away from him.

"Hi again. Can I help you?" replied Nigel.

"Yes, you can. Get out!" boomed shiny shoes, with Nigel jumping to his feet and heading straight for the door. "Calm down man, it's a joke. I've booked this room from 11. I was just wondering if you had finished.

"Oh, yes. I get it." Although Nigel didn't see how it was funny in any way. Nigel thought he had better show his appreciation for the joke by putting on a fake laugh and then saying "Very funny" before turning and leaving the room and letting shiny shoes take control of the meeting room.

Nigel headed back to his desk and carried on with the update and setup process. This might take the rest of the day to complete, but he should be in a good place in the morning to get the parts ordered.

After what seemed like the hundredth time an update had installed and the server rebooted, Nigel stood up from his desk to stretch his legs. He thought he might go and get a coffee, but when he looked around the room he noticed that most of the desks in the office were empty. Nigel checked the clock, it was half five. He had been so caught up in what he was doing that he hadn't noticed the time. For once, his day hadn't dragged and seem to last a week.

He grabbed his coat and headed for the doors, walked down the stairs to reception and left the building, starting his walk home.

FAMILY CATCH UP

I t was Tuesday evening. In Nigel's routine this meant that he should expect a call from his Mum and Dad around 7, which would normally last well over an hour. His Mum called it the catch up call, where she would ask what he had been up to, to which he would reply, "You know, not much, working as usual" and then his mum would spend the rest of the phone call telling him all about her week, before moving on to the weird things the neighbour's cats did and how the postman gets later every day and they are never as good as they used to be.

Then at the end of the hour Dave would ask how Dad was and his Dad would reply "Overworked and underpaid as usual", but Nigel knew that meant he was ok. Nigel was always reassured by his Dad's usual saying. He would know something wasn't right if he had replied, "Everything's fine".

It had been a long time since Nigel had seen his parents in person. He kept meaning to go and visit them, but somehow never got round to it. When Nigel was a student he would visit at least once a term. This would also coincide with him running out of clothes that could be worn without offending people 3 meters away with the smell. As well as him running out of money and having to make a withdrawal from the bank of mum and dad.

Once Nigel had got his new job and his own place, he had grown out of his student lifestyle and had learnt how to operate a washing machine all by himself, as well as how to budget his money. During one of his reading sessions one evening he stumbled-upon stumbled-upon which had a link to a money saving website. This had loads of information about how to shop online and how to save money with online voucher codes. When his new washing machine was delivered it had a strange square barcode on it, and after a little research found an app on his phone to scan it. This then led him to the manufacturer's YouTube channel with a multitude of informative videos about what liquid goes where and what powder is needed for each type of wash. As I said, Nigel didn't have much to do apart from learning from the internet.

Anyway, this meant that Nigel hadn't needed to visit his parents anymore, but now he realised he actually wanted to visit them. He would make sure he would arrange a weekend to go back home and visit soon in the phone call.

Nigel opened his fridge and took out his previously purchased microwave meal, but then decided to put it back in the fridge. He realised that he was not just stuck in a rut with his work routine, but also his home routine. He had the same meal routine each week, which offered a variation of flavours throughout the days of the week, as well as healthy balanced diet. It was easy.

He went shopping every Saturday morning and picked up the same meals from the shop down the road every shopping trip. He would walk into the shop, pick up a basket, walk to the refrigerated section and then work his way along from left to right, picking up one of each of the seven varieties of meals. He used to check the meals as he picked them up, but by now he realised that the shopkeeper had a stronger case of OCD than he did so he needn't bother. He was in and out of the shop in less than five minutes, after the less organised walk through the aisles for his cereals, milk and specialist coffee.

That was a good point. Nigel had been working so hard he hadn't stopped for the usual coffee breaks today. He fired up his coffee machine and made himself one of the best smelling coffee's he had ever had. Well, that's not entirely true. There was his first ever coffee he had had on holiday in Italy with his parents.

The trip to Italy was his parent's idea to show him more of the world before he left for University. It was designed to show him that the world is a great big place and full of different people and opportunities. Well, that's what they said to his face, but Nigel had overheard them talking in the kitchen when they thought he was out of earshot, that it will help him grow up and turn him into an adult and realise the world is a difficult place where you have to work hard for a living.

The trip started with the drive to the airport and loads of traffic, then a queue for parking, followed by what seemed like a continuous walking queue through check in, security and boarding. His Dad never said much but Nigel could hear him muttering to himself.

"Bloody queues." and "Come on", as well as "And they call this a holiday!". Nigel's Mum overheard the last one and looked at his Dad with the fakest, forced smile you have ever seen and said "What was that dear?", to which his Dad replied "Oh, um, I can't wait for this holiday!" whilst gritting his teeth and attempting a smile at the same time.

Anyway, the holiday continued in such a manner, queuing onto the plane, flying and queueing off the plane, followed by a reverse of the UK airport, before queueing to catch the coach to the resort. The resort was just as manic with everyone rushing to check in, before heading to the rooms to change into their swimming costumes and heading straight for the pool, which of course meant some angry arguments with some Germans and Russians over the sun beds.

Nigel's Mum and Dad thought this was the perfect kind of hell to show Nigel what the real world was like. Soon he would be heading off to University and once that was finished he had to escape his bubble of Mum and Dad's protection and fend for himself.

Nigel however, knowing his parent's plan, decided that he would use this situation for his advantage. He decided to go exploring.

"I'm a bit tired from the traveling, I think I'm going to go lie down for a bit" lied Nigel. His parents looked at each other and winked at each other thinking their plan was already working a treat. They were less than subtle though and Nigel saw this, but pretended he didn't see it before walking off towards the hotel. Nigel walked in through the front doors, but rather than heading for the lift he headed straight through the lobby and outside into the outside world.

Strangely, outside the hotel was actually a lot quieter, without all the hustle and bustle of the pool.

The hotel was on the edge of a sleepy small town, where the main road to the hotel was designed for coaches back and forth from the airport, but the road after that which led to the town itself narrowed down to a single track road. Nigel decided that the short walk to the town would be a great place to start his exploration.

Nigel walked the short distance, but he felt like he was transported from the 21st century, back in time to a medieval village, with narrow cobbled streets and houses built from stone. He walked through the town, turning left and right as the streets wound themselves around the old buildings. He turned a corner and suddenly there was a wide open space of the town square (later from his reading online he would learn the term piazza). There were a few people walking through the square on their way as well as a few people sat down at some tables and chairs in the corner of the square. Nigel walked over to the chairs and sat down to admire the buildings that surrounded the square.

No sooner had he sat down there was a beautiful young Italian woman stood next to him with a pen and notepad. Nigel was unsure where she had appeared from but he suddenly realised this must have been a cafe. This suddenly made Nigel realise he didn't know any Italian. Maybe exploring without his Mum and Dad wasn't the greatest idea.

The lady, the waitress, looked at him and started speaking in Italian to him. Nigel had no idea what she had said, not that he could really concentrate on what she was saying as he was staring into her beautiful dark eyes. Nigel always liked the sound of foreign accents, especially Italian.

Now, there are two ways that British people in other countries can behave when it comes to communicating in the native language. They can either start shouting in English whilst subconsciously playing charades to try and explain themselves, or they can smile and nod. Nigel went with the smiling and nodding option.

The waitress smiled back and then turned and walked into a doorway of what looked like a house, but Nigel assumed was the inside of the cafe. Nigel was again alone and decided to admire the architecture of the buildings of the square again.

The waitress returned a couple of minutes later and had a coffee cup on a tray, which she then placed carefully on the table in front of Nigel, before smiling at him and then walking back into the house style cafe.

Nigel was a tea drinker and had never really tried coffee before, but he thought he might as well try it, and he didn't want to offend the beautiful waitress. He picked up the cup and took a sip.

Wow.

The combination of the frothy milk with the strong, bold tasting coffee was amazing. This was the start of a beautiful friendship between Nigel and coffee. All other coffee would have to try and live up to this cup. He wasn't sure if it was because of the coffee itself, or the amazing surroundings, or being served by the beautiful Italian waitress. Nigel decided to himself that it was a perfect combination of the three.

Nigel slowly sipped his coffee, trying to make the experience last as long as possible, watching the few people in the town go about their business. Eventually though he had finished the cup and put it back down onto the table.

Nigel wasn't sure what to do next. He wanted to sit and enjoy the town for as long as possible but was scared but also strangely excited by the fact the waitress would be returning in the near future. Not knowing what to say to her he took out a few euros from his pocket and put them on the coffee cup saucer and made a break for it before she returned to more embarrassment than the first meeting.

Nigel walked around the town and found another single track road out into the countryside. He walked along the road into the lush Italian countryside filled with fields of crops and vineyards. Nigel realised that this was the countryside that he had wanted to see and kept walking for over an hour, getting further and further from the tourist hotspot of the hotel.

Whilst Nigel was having the time of his life exploring on his adventure, his Mum and Dad were not. The kids at the pool decided to have a water fight right next to Nigel's Mums sunbed, which as you can probably guess, ended up with a bucket of cold water splashing over her legs. Nigel's Mum did what anyone would do and screamed a high pitch scream and threw her hands into the air.

Just as Nigel's Mum threw her hands into the air a poolside waiter was walking by with the crate of ice from the hotel and delivering it to the poolside bar for the lunch time cocktail special. Her hands, and probably not helped by the scream, caught the waiter off guard and caused the heavy crate to slip out of his hands, spilling the contents of the crate, with half going on the floor and half going all over Nigel's Mum and Dad.

More screams then followed.

Nigel's Mum and Dad jumped into the air with shock, not realising the floor was now covered in ice, leading them to slip into each other and then falling as if in slow motion into the cold pool with a massive splash.

The children having the water fight thought this was fantastic. They laughed out loud (or lol'd as kids say these days) and then decided to fill their buckets with the ice of the floor and carry on their fight around the pool area throwing ice over the rest of the guests.

Eventually, Nigel's Mum and Dad got themselves out of the pool, gathered their sopping wet belongings and headed back to their hotel room to recover, leaving the pool staff trying to resolve the pandemonium that was all around them.

This is when things started to go wrong for Nigel and caused a turning point in his life. Upon discovering that Nigel wasn't in his room his Mum and Dad panicked and called the hotel reception who called the police, mainly after Nigel's mum's panicked shouting of "My baby! Where has my baby gone? My poor little Nigel all alone in a foreign country!", leaving the hotel staff to think a young child had been abducted.

Within minutes the blue flashing lights of the police cars had arrived at the hotel and police radio broadcasts were being sent all over the region to be on the lookout for a young boy called Nigel.

It would be over an hour before a translator would arrive at the hotel to take the description of the boy from his Mum and Dad and only at that point the police were made aware that the child was actually a teenager and not a young child after all.

Nigel was walking down the lane between fields in peace and quiet, until all of a sudden he heard the siren of a police car coming towards him. Instinctively he stood to one side of the road as the sound got closer, just in time for the police car to come rushing around the corner towards him. The car rushed past, but then slammed on its brakes and came to a halt in a cloud of dust.

Before the dust cleared the car started reversing back towards him and stopped near him. Two police officers rushed out and stood either side of Nigel, forcing him to back up towards the car.

"Nigel?" Asked the taller of the two police officers, in his Italian accent.

It took a few seconds for Nigel to understand what the police office had said before he replied "Yes, I'm Nigel".

The two officers pounced and turned Nigel so he faced towards the car, pushed him forward so his body and face hit the car with a thud. Before he knew it, Nigel was in handcuffs and being forced into the back of the car. The car then sped off back towards the town and the hotel, sirens blazing.

Back at the hotel Nigel's mum was a shivering wreck. She had only stopped sobbing long enough for the translator to get Nigel's description before starting again. Nigel's dad was trying his best to console her, with phrases like "there, there" and "I'm sure he's fine. He's probably got lost and fallen down somewhere" which just made the situation worse.

A siren brought everyone to a stop and Nigel's mum stopped wailing long enough to see what was going on. The police car ground to a halt outside the hotel and the two police officers got out and then opened the back door and got Nigel out.

Nigel's mum stood up and started rushing towards him, out of the hotel doors and into the Italian sunshine. But just before she reached him the police officers turned Nigel around to release his handcuffs. Nigel's mum saw the handcuffs and then stopped still.

Her demeanour suddenly changed from a sad, sobbing woman, to an extremely angry and embarrassed mother.

"What have you done! What were you thinking! Where did you go!" She bellowed.

Nigel went to start talking but by then Nigel's Dad had caught up.

"Your mother and I were worried sick! Where the hell were you?" Shouted Nigel's Dad.

Nigel opened his mouth to reply that he just went for a walk but his mum and dad had turned their attention to the police and were singing their praises for finding him so quickly and that they were sorry for whatever he had done and that he was an only child that had never been out of Britain before and doesn't know what he is doing.

Nigel, now out of handcuffs, started walking back towards the hotel, feeling extremely embarrassed. Just before he went through the lobby doors he turned around to see the police car zooming off and his parents stood next to the kerb hugging each other. He knew his parents would never let him forget this and that would be the end to his explorations this holiday and until he went to University. He would not be let out of his parents site. He didn't think it would be any worse but then he saw the beautiful waitress from the cafe in the crowd and felt even more embarrassed than before.

From this point on it was drilled into him not to explore, be cautious, play it safe.

It had affected him more than he had realised, but now life had given him a new opportunity.

SPECIAL DELIVERY

The next day at work Nigel was ready to order his list of spare parts. The server had finished downloading it's missing updates and was now ready to use. He had the dusty manual in his hands and was working through the instructions step by step.

"Ahem!"

Nigel turned round, still looking down from reading the manual, seeing a pair of shiny shoes, before looking up to see Mr Shiny Shoes looking at him. Before Nigel could say "good morning" shiny shoes started talking at him. Not to him, at him.

"What's all these alert emails I've just got?" Said shiny shoes.

"Umm, I don't know? What do they say?" Replied Nigel.

"They say intranet alert and some of them go back years?"

"Oh right." Said Nigel as he thought of something to say "I've just run some updates on the server so it must be a bug in the update." He lied. He couldn't turn round and say it's because he had only just plugged in and turned on the server after working here all these years.

"Computers eh? Can't live with them, can't live without them. Get on to head office and let them know it's on the blink" said shiny shoes as he turned and walked smugly back to his office.

He hadn't anticipated issues like this with all of his excitement at getting the server going yesterday. He had better read the manual more thoroughly and check what would happen when he placed the order. It might trigger a workflow and automatically send emails around the company, placing him in the spotlight.

This was not going to be as easy as he had first thought. Oh well, best get on with the reading then.

Nigel spent until lunch time reading through the rest of the manual and had identified a few potential issues.

If he was to place an order then it would need to be approved by someone, but luckily Nigel could log on to the server directly as the admin and approve it directly. There was a process that the administrator could follow to free up any blocked orders in the system and Nigel could use this himself.

The delivery would arrive within a week from headquarters by courier so he would have to ensure he spoke to whichever random receptionist was there on that day so that she called him directly for the parcel and not just call anyone to come and get it.

The next issue is that the maximum order value was £10,000. The list that Dave had given Nigel didn't seem that big, but once Nigel had researched the part numbers on the intranet he realised that these were not cheap spare parts as Dave had explained to him. One part was a camera lens, but it was a specialist lens for a 360 degree camera. This cost £5,000 on its own!

He could avoid the maximum order value by placing several orders over a matter of days, ensuring he manually approved each order. But he had to decide if one large value order would be less visible than several small orders.

The camera that went with the lens was £15,000 on its own so there was no way he could order it himself. That needed to be ordered directly by the head of sales and marketing, Mr Shiny

Shoes himself.

Nigel was now regretting agreeing to this business venture. He thought that no one would notice a few spare parts going missing but now he understood the value of the parts he was sure he would get caught. He had to speak to Dave.

He opened his calendar and arranged a meeting with Dave in the meeting room for 2pm that day, hoping Dave would accept and he could update him on his issues.

Dave quickly accepted the meeting request and Nigel went to get a coffee whilst he thought about how to word his concerns.

"So we meet again!" began Dave as he walked into the meeting room, closing the door behind him. "Two meetings in a week. People will start talking about us!"

Nigel hadn't known Dave for very long but he should have expected an opening like this. It threw him off guard and now he had forgotten his practiced speech. Instead his mind was thinking of a comeback. But as usual Nigel just responded with an "Uhh".

Dave started laughing at Nigels response. "Strangely, it seems your mind works faster when you're drunk. Maybe you should sneak some whiskey into your coffee!"

"Good one." Nigel said as he tried to regain his composure and remember why he had called the meeting. "I needed to speak to you about these parts you want to order. I don't think it's going to work. They are too expensive and I think people will notice."

"Too expensive? How much are they?" replied Dave, looking slightly concerned, but then quickly returned to his smile.

"Well, the lens you have asked for is £15 grand and the system needs that to be approved by the Sales and Marketing manager. I can work around some of the other issues but that one is just going to be too difficult to resolve." Nigel spoke ever quicker with each word. "It will flag up then they will look into what else has been ordered and start working out something is going on. They we will be out of a job and headed to prison for theft."

"Woah, woah, woah Nigel. Steady on there." Dave reassured Nigel "It may seem like a lot of money for regular folk but this company makes billions of pounds each year and sells thousands of these products all over the world. I'm sure they won't notice a few parts going missing from here and there. There is a problem, so we just need to be creative and think of a solution."

Suddenly something in Nigel's head clicked. Dave said the products are available all over the world. He had been looking at the order prices for the UK, maybe he could look at prices in other countries and do something with exchange rates to lower the value below the approval threshold. Maybe he could make the worldwide market work in his favour, spreading the orders around to different countries so that no one saw the complete order, just small parts.

"I've had an idea. Got to go." said Nigel as he stood up and hurried out of the meeting room, leaving Dave sat there on his own wondering what was going on, but happy that Nigel had found a potential solution to their problem.

Nigel returned to his desk and looked at the manual and flipped to the index. He remembered there was a page with the intranet sites for the other countries, opening each in a new tab in his browser. He searched for the lens in each before he found the price he needed in the Hong Kong intranet site. Delivery would be longer, but the price, after exchange rate was £9,980. Below the £10k approval threshold! He then started searching for different parts from the list in different countries and started placing the orders. He estimated that in a week he would have all the parts he needed, without any approval from Shiny shoes.

Don't try and beat the system, make the system work for you!

ASSEMBLY LINE

The week after the orders were placed all the items had arrived. Ordering from around the world also helped stagger the delivery dates so they didn't all come at once. There also seemed to be a different receptionist each day of the week so they didn't notice Nigel collecting so many packages from reception over the week.

Most of the parts were small enough for Nigel to fit into his satchel, or man bag as the kids outside the corner shop called it when he went in, so Nigel had taken them home each night.

Nigel waited for Dave to go into the kitchen at work and followed him in, looking around to make sure no one else was in the kitchen before he started talking to him. Nigel snuck up behind Dave as he was making himself a cup of tea. "That's all the parts from your list here now. What's the plan now?"

Dave turned round and said a bit too loudly "Morning Nigel, how are you?" turning his head to look across the office before grinning back at him.

"Yeah, um, Good morning." said Nigel.

"That was for that nosy cow on the desk next to mine. Always trying to stick her nose in and eavesdrop all my phone calls." Dave said in a more hushed tone. "She's not looking now. What were you saying?"

"All the parts are here now. What's the next step in the plan?" asked Nigel.

"Well, now we have to play mad scientist and construct our monster" replied Dave. "Have you got some room at your place? Mine is a bt too cluttered to be building something like this."

"Well, yeah. There's room on the table. We can build it there if you like?" said Nigel

"Great, I'll come round yours tonight and we can get started. Better go now, that nosey cow is looking over here again, you think she would try and be a bit more subtle about it!" Dave walked out of the kitchen and back into the office. As he got to his desk he asked the girl at the desk next to his if there was anything he could help her with before she tutted and looked back at her screen again.

Nigel walked home quicker than usual, worried he wouldn't have enough time to tidy up before Dave got there later in the evening. He got to his front door and unlocked it, and walked in to his immaculate living room as tidy as it always was. Nigel then realised he shouldn't have worried about tidying. His house was always spotlessly clean, the advantage of not having a social life.

Nigel moved all of the packages onto the table in the living room and then went and made himself one of his premium coffees whilst he waited for Dave to turn up.

There was a knock at the door at half seven. Nigel walked to the door and opened it, to see Dave there with his slicked back hair, wearing his jeans and a t shirt. Nigel suddenly realised he was still in his office wear. Nigel didn't have a lot of non office clothes, but he thought to himself he would rather be wearing this than his recently acquired leather trousers.

Dave looked at Nigel as he opened the door.

"Evening Nigel" said Dave, "I wasn't sure if you would be opening the door, or if it would be your butler."

"Butler?" replied Nigel.

"I half expected you to be wearing a smoking jacket and waiting for me in your drawing room." Dave continued, "Its a nice area of town you live in here mate, bit better than where I call home."

Nigel hadn't really thought about his part of town for a while. He had just gotten used to it. Of course, when he was looking for a place to live before he moved in he had done extensive online research and had set up instant alerts on his phone as soon as properties became available in this area of town. He had looked at lots of different parts of town which he had then graded from great, to average and then below average. Nigel wasn't satisfied with below average or even average, so he focused on the great areas.

Despite all of the technology at his disposal and all the alerts it was a coincidence that he found his current house. On one of his research walks around the great areas he walked past the house just as a light came on and caught his attention. He instinctively looked in the window and saw the person inside sticking a 'To Let' sign up in the window. There was no one else in the street so Nigel saw this as too much of a coincidence and knocked on the door and started speaking to the owner there and then. The owner was moving to the Costa Brava and wanted to rent his house out, but didn't want to get involved in estate agent fees. A deal was struck and Nigel moved in a couple of weeks later.

"I got a good deal on the rent and the owner hasn't asked for an increase since" replied Nigel. In fact, now that Nigel had thought about it, he hadn't spoken to his landlord in a long time. "Come on in. Did you want a coffee?"

"Coffee? Nah, I brought some beers over for us" Dave said, as he raised a carrier bag up for Nigel to see. "All work and no play, as they say."

Dave came into the house and walked into the living room, putting the bag down on the table, next to the packages. He immediately started ripping the boxes apart to get to the delicate electronics contained inside. He threw the packaging into a pile on the floor, upsetting Nigel's perfectly clean and ordered living room, concentrating only on the parts, identifying which part is which purely by sight, ignoring the labels. He then strategically placed the parts in some sort of order on the table.

"Do us a favour Nigel and get us a glass for a beer. Help yourself as well if you want one." Dave said, without taking his focus off the parts.

Nigel had never seen anyone so focused as Dave. He was like a man possessed, no longer the laid back character he had grown to know. It seemed to Nigel as if Dave had been practising this moment in his head over and over again, knowing how each part should connect to the other to create his contraption.

Nigel went into the kitchen and got a couple of glasses out of the cupboard, before returning to the living room, where he found Dave pulling a soldering iron out of the bag that contained the beer. Without asking, Dave found a socket and plugged the soldering iron in and sat it on the table to warm up.

Nigel put the glasses down on the coffee table and pulled a couple of cans out of the bag. They were not what he was used to or what he expected. Budget lager. Nigel didn't say anything, he just poured them into the glasses, before taking the other cans back into the fridge.

When Nigel returned to the living room again Dave now had a soldering iron in his right hand and sipping from a the glass of lager in the left. Dave didn't talk again for half an hour, just focused intensely on the task at hand. Nigel stood behind him watching, captivated on Dave's assembly work.

Dave finally broke the silence, but only to ask Nigel if he could get him another pint.

After another 30 minutes, and another pint finished, Dave stood up and stretched.

"Just need to use the men's room" said Dave as he walked off and upstairs.

This gave Nigel a chance to look at what Dave had been doing in more detail. There seemed to be two parts to the device. On the left side of the table was a makeshift headset with two screens and wires coming out of it. It looked functional, but like it needed a bit of refinement and style.

On the other side of the table was a pair of glasses with a wire coming out of the back of one side and into a small box. Nigel was unsure why a VR system would need two headsets to work, especially as the second had no screens attached, but then he noticed a tiny camera had been attached to the glasses and the wire that came out of the back of the glasses.

Nigel picked up the glasses and tried them on. They felt just like a normal set of glasses. He put them down and then picked up the VR headset and put them on. It took a couple of seconds for his eyes to adjust to the screens before he realised that he was looking at his own living room.

It was then that Nigel felt a hand on his shoulder that made him jump, causing the headset to slip down his nose. Nigel grabbed it before it slipped any further and put it back onto the table.

"Woah, woah, woah, careful with the merchandise!" joked Dave.

"Sorry, I was just having a look" replied Nigel.

"Quite an immersive experience, eh?" asked Dave.

"Yeah, just confused me looking at my living room?" Nigel commented.

"Well, there's good reason for that" began Dave "You said to me in the pub that the issue with VR is the software, so my idea is not to use any."

Nigel was confused and he obviously displayed the confused look on his face, as Dave carried on talking.

"People so far have made virtual worlds for virtual reality, but they don't realise that no matter how good the software is, it will never be real. Therefore, why not give people an experience they can't experience in the real world." explained Dave.

Nigel was now even more confused than he was before and he was sure this was showing on his face to Dave again. He tried to make sense of it and started talking out loud.

"So, it's not virtual reality. It's just reality?" asked Nigel, "So you are giving people a real life live feed."

Nigel suddenly remembered a film he had watched, many years ago. His Mum was watching it on TV and he wasn't really paying attention but it came back to him now for some reason.

"Victor Victoria" Nigel muttered under his breath quietly.

"What's that Nigel? Speak up" said Dave.

"Well, it just reminded me of a film I watched once. I mean it's kind of a similar concept, just without drag queens, and with technology, well, kind of" replied Nigel.

Dave burst out laughing. "Drag queens? You learn something new about you every day Nigel. You do keep surprising me".

"Sorry, I didn't explain that very well, did I?" Nigel replied. "Basically the plot is there is a lady called Victoria who can't get a job as a performer as the popular acts are men playing women. So they come up with this plan to have a woman, pretending to be a man, pretending to be a woman."

Dave looked confused for a second but then got where Nigel was going with this.

"So our virtual reality is real life, pretending to be virtual reality, pretending to be real?" Nigel said, nodding his head in approval. "I like that analogy. It's a good way of thinking about it. Just with less drag queens".

Both Dave and Nigel smiled.

"That reminds me, one thing we are missing is a name. Let's call it Project Victor!" they both nodded in agreement.

"So, all we need to do now is to work out a control method so the user can control the person wearing the glasses." finished Dave.

"What? So who will be wearing the glasses?" asked Nigel.

"Well, me or you" replied Dave, "But like I said, we've got some more work to do before we get there. We need to work out a controls method."

This triggered something in Nigel's memory. An article about people using games controllers to map 3D space.

"We need a Wii." said Nigel.
"I've just been mate?" said Dave.

"What? No I mean a Wii. A Nintendo Wii" clarified Nigel.

"I, just thought we could use the controllers for our project. If the user holds a controller in each hand to control the person wearing the glasses arms." Nigel finished.

"That might just work" replied Dave "Good idea. See, great team work!"

Nigel opened the drawer under his TV unit and pulled out an old Wii console and the controllers and handed it to Dave. Dave immediately started taking the unit to pieces and laid out the disassembled components across the table. Somehow he knew what components he needed and picked them out of, what looked to Nigel, a tangle of wires and elements.

Dave carried on assembling pieces whilst Nigel stood by and watched. He had no idea what Dave was doing but Dave seemed to be 100% focused on the task at hand and didn't stop until he had used all the pieces he had stripped from the console.

"I think the sensors are almost there now." Dave said.

Nigel looked at the assembled product. The pair of glasses that had the screens in now had a long wire coming from each side with a sensor on the end. Each sensor had a strap from a Wii controller to attach it to the wearers wrist so they could move their arms without fear of the sensor falling off.

"Now we just need to figure out how to convey the movements from the sensors to the wearer of the other headset?" said Dave.

Nigel suddenly remembered reading something about helicopter pilots and them getting confused about which way is up and down when they are flying around with lots of dust.

"Not sure if this will work, but I remember reading something about using things that vibrate in helicopter pilots suits. When they get disoriented different parts of the suit vibrate to help them level the helicopter without using their eyes." replied Nigel.

"Yeah, that could work. Different amounts of vibration in each direction to signify the direction to move" finished Dave.

Dave found some more parts he needed from the Wii remotes and began his construction frenzy once more.

After another half hour Dave stopped what he was doing and stepped back to admire his handy work.
The second pair of glasses with the camera also had a wire coming out of each side with a wristband attached to the end of each, except this had four small components attached to each wristband instead of the sensor.

"Right then Nigel, put on these glasses and put these straps around the wrists." said Dave

Nigel picked up the glasses and put them on before putting his hands through the wrist straps, adjusting them until they felt comfortable on him.

Dave then picked up the other pair of glasses with the screens and put them on the top of his head whilst he put the wristbands with the motion sensors on his wrists. Once they were comfortable he slid the glasses down over his eyes.

"Right, I can see what you can see. See if you can match my arm movements." Dave paused before continuing, "The writstbands should vibrate so try and move your arms in the direction they vibrate, so if the top vibrates, move your arms up."

"Ok let's see how this works" replied Nigel, excited to see what would happen.

Dave started moving his left arm up and down slowly. Nigel felt the left wrist band vibrating, first on the top of the wrist indicating the upward movement, before vibrating underneath his wrist to indicate a downward movement. Nigel moved his arm in the direction of the vibration, trying to keep in sync with the feed of controls Dave was sending.

Dave started moving his right arm from left to right, and Nigel's right wrist vibrated accordingly so he moved that wrist to match the vibration.

"Right, it looks like you have the basics. Let's try something a bit more complicated. This will be fun" said Dave, with a smile forming on his face.

Dave moved both his hands in front of him with the palms facing down. Nigel copied the movement based on the sensor feedback. Dave then turned his hands palm up, right then left. Again Nigel copied. Next Dave moved his right hand onto his left shoulder, before placing his left hand onto his right shoulder. Again Nigel copied. Dave moved his right hand onto his right hip before moving his left hand onto his left hip. Nigel copied again, but now Nigel was smiling too. He knew where this was going.

"Hey Macarena" Nigel shouted out loud continuing the dance, before both of them burst into fits of laughter.

"I wasn't sure if you would get that one." said Nigel through the laughter. "You're a natural at this"

Nigel hadn't had this much fun for a very long time. He was trying to think back to the last time he had danced the Macarena. It was before he started working at Amstaria that's for sure. It was probably back at university in one of the freshers week parties, one of those parties where you paid a tenner to get in and drink as much as you wanted, before you were thrown out or passed out and then thrown out.

Nigel thought back to that party, or what he could remember of it anyway. He remembered slowly sipping a bottle of beer in the corner on his own whilst everyone else was on the dance floor. He was planning on drinking his beer before slipping out of the door without his university halls room mates noticing, but then his plan was scuppered by one of the clubs reps who was walking round the club handing out shots of vodka.

Nigel had enjoyed a beer or two but had never ventured into spirits before. His Mum and Dad always told him to be careful with what he drank and never to drink spirits.

"Shots for everyone! No exceptions!" the club rep said to him before handing him a shot of vodka.

"Ahh, no thanks" said Nigel "I uhh, don't drink…"

"Come on mate, get it down ya, one shot won't hurt." interrupted the rep. "If you never try it how do you know if you like it?"

The rep poured himself a shot as well and raised it in front of him. Nigel replicated the action, still unsure whether to drink or not, before a highly attractive blonde student saw the two of them, wanting to join in.

"Oooh shots! Let's have one then!" said the attractive blond student.

The rep was happy to oblige, pouring her a shot, before they all raised their glasses in front of their faces again, ready to drink the shot. Nigel didn't mind looking stupid in front of the rep, but now with the blonde student there as well, the peer pressure suddenly took on a new level. Nigel thought to himself, "What the hell", as the rep started counting down, "3, 2, 1" before the three of them downed their shots.

Nigel's throat instantly burned and he let out a long cough, whilst turning his head to the side, shutting his eyes.

"Let's have another!" said the blonde student, with the rep happy to oblige, pouring three more shots out, handing the two shots out to the others keeping one for himself.

"3, 2, 1" said the rep, before Nigel had even recovered from the first shot he found himself downing another. He had the same burning reaction as the first shot, but this time he knew what to expect and had a slightly more controlled reaction.

Before he knew what was happening they had two more shots, before the blonde student grabbed the rep and Nigel's hands and dragged them to the dance floor. The rep smiled and winked at Nigel thinking he was on to a winner with the blonde. They joined the crowded dance floor and danced and danced, with the vodka entering Nigels blood system, before the dj played the Macarena. Nigel had never danced that dance before but the blonde student, as well as everyone else on the dance floor, seemed to know what to do. He started copying everyone else and by the end of the routine he considered himself an expert. Maybe it was just the vodka but he was having a great time.

"More shots!" shouted Nigel and the rep was happy to oblige once more. The night slowly went down hill from there, with Nigel being thrown out of the club about three in the morning, singing "Heeey Macarena" as loud as he can all the way home to his University halls.

Nigel woke up with the mother of all hangovers the next morning, or rather afternoon to be exact.

"It's getting late" said Dave, bringing Nigel back to the present.

"Yeah, time flies when you are having fun" smiled Nigel.

"Time to call it a night" said Dave and he took his glasses and wristbands off as Nigel did the same.

"Is it ok if I leave this all here? I don't really have space for all this at my place" Dave asked.

"Yeah, no problem." Nigel replied.

Nigel got a spare box out from one of his cupboards and Dave and Nigel packed away the wires as neatly as they could.

"I think we've made some good progress tonight" said Dave with a smile.

"Yeah, I'm pretty amazed to be honest. Where did you learn to build stuff like that?" Nigel asked.

"You know, just picked it up as I go along really." said Dave. "Right, see you later!"

With that, Dave made for the door before Nigel could get any more detailed answers from Dave.

Nigel locked the door behind Dave, turned the lights off and headed off to bed.

THE ALPHA RELEASE

Nigel spent the next day at work continuing to read through and set up the rest of the intranet server. Now that he had actually plugged it in he thought he might as well learn to use it and see what it did. It might come in handy one day and, to be honest, it was a welcome distraction from thinking about the device that they had created the previous night and what the next step was.

Nigel still had no idea how Dave had assembled it and even where he had learned all those electronics manufacturing skills. Nigel was useless with anything to do with hardware, as you could probably tell by the amount of time it took him to realise there was a server sat on his desk that needed plugging in. He could do basic things like setting up a surround sound system, but most of that was configuring options through the on screen menus. The hardware set up basically involved plugging coloured wires into the matching coloured socket, so as long as you weren't colour blind, anyone should be able to do it.

Nigel always had a way with settings and configurations, getting the best out of a system. A lot of this skill came from when his Mum and Dad used to buy new electronic devices and attempt to set them up. He would come home from school and see his parents randomly jabbing buttons on the front of the new electronic device trying to get it to do something.

It would normally start with his Mum and Dad ripping open the box and removing everything out of its packaging and plugging in wires in the back in the holes that fitted the cable and then expecting it to work straight away. The ripped up packaging and manuals would be scooped up into a bin bag ready to be taken out to the bin, whereupon Nigel would then carefully remove the manual and start reading it. Once he had read the first few pages he would approach the new electronic device that was still being poked and prodded by his parents.

"Press that one" said his Mum.

"I've tried that one. It doesn't do anything." replied his Dad. "Maybe its this one?"

"I told you to pay for the fitting service. You never listen to me..." began his Mum.

"They shouldn't make it so difficult. Its their plan to get you to pay for the fitting. It's a joke!" interrupted Dad. "Its no good. It'll have to go back to the shop!"

"But you've ripped all the packaging now, they won't take it back now." said Mum before tutting under her breath.

"They will have to take it back! It's broken isn't it!" Nigel's Dad replied getting a bit louder with each sentence.

"Have you tried the switch on the back?" said Nigel, seeing his chance to diffuse the situation, before the device was ripped off the shelf, with wires snapping and sparks flying.

His Dad looked at him for a couple of seconds, acknowledging his presence for the first time, before looking at the back of the device and spotting the switch, flicking it to the on position.

The device suddenly lit up and burst into life.

"Well, I'm sure I tried that earlier" said Nigel's Dad, confused. "How did you know to do that?"

"Well, in the manual it says…" began Nigel.

"Oh there's a manual?" said Nigel's Mum. "Where was that? We didn't see one when we opened the box?"

"Well done Nigel, that sorted it." said Nigel's Dad, "But you know Nigel, life doesn't come with a manual. Sometimes you just have to live life and work it out yourself."

That was one of his Dad's popular sayings. He didn't see the need for manuals and instructions. If he couldn't figure something out in an hour then he wasn't meant to use it.

Nigel never really understood that saying as if you want to know how something worked, you read the manual and it told you what to do. Maybe it was a generation difference, where his parents grew up without the internet so if they got stuck with something they had to figure it out themselves or ask someone else for help.

If Nigel had a problem when he was growing up he could access the internet and do a search. Normally someone else had the same problem and wrote a blog post about it, responded to a question on a forum or created a video about it on YouTube.

But the project with Dave had no instructions. It had no blog posts and no videos on YouTube to help them out. The only way was to try it out and see what happens. They would have to do an alpha test in the real world and just go for it. They would have to make their own instruction manual as they went along and learn from their mistakes.

Nigel's attention was brought back to the computer screen by a flashing message appearing in the bottom right of the screen.

The message read "Intranet chat has been successfully installed". One of the many server updates must have installed a messaging service onto the intranet server and it had just finished installing and configuring itself. Nigel thought he might as well test it out and see what it did.

He opened up the chat service and familiarised himself with the layout. It seemed pretty simple to use. There was a list of employees on the left and a chat window on the right. As Nigel had never bothered to learn anyone in the office's names the list didn't really mean much to him. He scrolled through the list until he saw the name "Dave", pressed on it and started typing a message.

"Same time tonight?" and pressed send.

Nigel waited for a response to come back through the chat, but instead he was suddenly aware of feet stomping towards him in a hurry, followed by huffing and puffing. Nigel looked over his left shoulder and saw a pair of shiny shoes on the floor next to him.

"What the hell are you doing Nigel? Is this some kind of joke? Well I can tell you now its not funny and is completely inappropriate at work!" bellowed Shiny Shoes. "You are normally such a good worker keeping to yourself. I don't know what's gotten into you but this better be a one off or we will have to have words!"

With that Shiny Shoes turned and headed back to his office, still huffing and puffing along the way. Nigel realised the rest of the office were now silent and staring straight at him, wondering what the hell he had done to upset Shiny Shoes. After a few seconds the phones started ringing again and everyone got back to their work, whatever it was they did.

Well, at least Nigel had learnt Shiny Shoes was called Dave. Nigel turned back to the screen and right clicked on Dave and selected the 'Block Contact 'option to prevent any further miscommunication issues.

Nigel scrolled down the list again and saw there were no more Dave's but the was a David. This had to be the right one this time. This time he thought he would try a more generic welcome message to start off the conversation, just in case.

"Hi Dave, how's it going?"

"ROFL! What u do?" came the reply after a few minutes. Nigel knew it was the correct Dave this time.

"Tell you later. Just wanted to know when are we meeting again?"

"Tonite?" came the reply

Nigel was going to reply "You mean 'tonight'" but thought better of it. He didn't want to turn into one of those grammar bullies on social media, and anyway, online chat is supposed to be fun and trendy, or so he had read, not having much experience using it himself.

"Kewl, c u l8r" Nigel replied, following the trend.

Nigel got on with the rest of his day researching the latest updates to the Intranet server, excited as to what Dave had planned for later. Home time seemed to take ages to come, no matter what Nigel was reading. Previously, reading made his days go past quickly, blurring from one day to the next, but not anymore.

Home time finally came and Dave and Nigel got up from their chairs and headed off. Dave said "See you later" to Nigel as they left the building.

Nigel walked home and then cleared the table, making room for Project Victor. He then went upstairs to change into his casual clothes, which no longer required a choice of ripped jeans or leather trousers since Nigel had placed a few orders with an online clothes outlet since the evening at the pub.

He went down stairs and made himself some dinner, ate the dinner and then made himself one of his special coffees, before sitting down and waiting for Dave to knock on the door.

And he waited, and waited, and waited. Dave never came.

THE NO SHOW

Nigel walked in to work, got a coffee and sat down at his desk. He tried to make himself look busy whilst looking over his shoulder as often as possible looking for Dave, without cricking his neck or looking completely paranoid that he was being followed.

Dave eventually walked in to the office a few minutes past 9. His eyes were red and his normally slicked back hair looked a mess, as if he hadn't even bothered trying to style it this morning. His suit looked worse than normal too, not that it ever fitted properly in the first place, but he wasn't wearing a tie today and his shirt was untucked. He slouched into his chair and looked down at his feet, before shutting his eyes, seeming to force back tears.

The office door opened and Shiny Shoes came out to the kitchen and looked around to make sure everyone was working hard. He stopped in his tracks looking at Dave. Dave suddenly realised he was being looked at and quickly smoothed out his hair and tucked his shirt in, before getting his tie out of his pocket and started tying it around his neck. This seemed to satisfy Shiny Shoes who continued looking round the office, before stopping to look at Nigel this time.

Nigel realised he had been staring at Dave and Shiny Shoes too long, before quickly turning back to his desk and opening up the first program on his computer he could find and started typing to make himself look busy.

Shiny Shoes continued to the kitchen to get himself a coffee, feeling satisfied his presence in the office was being felt by the staff.

Nigel waited a few minutes for Shiny Shoes to return to his desk and then opened up the chat window.

"You Ok?" Nigel asked Dave.

No response.

"Everything ok? Can I help with anything?" sent Nigel.

After a few minutes a reply came through.

"Nah m8. L8r" Dave replied.

Nigel thought he had better leave it there. There was obviously something going on but Dave didn't want to talk about it. To Nigel, Dave was normally full of confidence and laughs, but today he saw a different side of him, like the wind had been taken out of his sails.

Another message came through to Nigel, all it said was "Lunch?". Nigel assumed this was an invitation to discuss things over lunch so he replied. "Sure, sounds good. Speak then"

The morning continued without incident, with both Dave and Nigel doing their best to concentrate on their work and avoid any more excuses for Shiny Shoes to glare at them.

At lunchtime Nigel followed Dave out of the office and onto the street outside. Dave didn't say anything and was looking down at the ground directly in front of him as he walked.

"What did you fancy for lunch then?" Nigel said, trying to break Dave from his malaise.

"You pick mate, whatever you fancy" Dave replied quietly, without looking up, continuing to walk.

"I know a good sandwich shop round the corner. They do a great roast chicken baguette" Nigel said, whilst thinking it was always pretty quiet in there so they would have space to talk without being overheard.

"Sure" replied Dave.

Nigel led the way to the sandwich shop. When they reached it and walked through the door, Dave went and sat down at a table in the corner, before looking down at his feet again, shutting his eyes as if trying to make something go away from his mind. Nigel looked at Dave for a few moments, wondering what he was about to be told, before going over to the counter and ordering two roast chicken baguettes to eat in. Nigel paid for the baguettes and then walked over to the table, sitting down opposite Dave.

Nigel sat patiently waiting for Dave to say something. He was still sat with his eyes closed, composing himself, so he could say what he needed to say. Dave took a deep breath and opened his eyes and began talking.

"I know you don't know a lot about me Nigel." Dave began, "We only met a few weeks ago but I feel I can trust you. You are a good friend."

The first bit was true, Nigel didn't know much about Dave and whenever he had asked questions, Dave had quickly changed the subject to something else. Nigel didn't mind. He kind of liked the aspect of mystery about Dave and his secrets. He always thought that Dave would open up when he was ready and never pushed him to answer questions. Dave was the first real friend Nigel had had in a long time and didn't want to risk upsetting the apple cart, but it looked like Dave was now ready to open up.

"I have, I mean, I had a brother, called Simon. He was my little brother but he was very ill for a long time. He had a disease where he was slowly losing control of his muscles and would become less mobile each day." Dave looked up to the ceiling and took another deep breath before continuing.

"He passed away last night in his sleep" Dave stopped talking now. Letting what he had just said sink in, as if by him saying it finally made it true and he couldn't lie to himself anymore.

"He was a fighter though. The doctors gave him a month when they finally diagnosed his condition but Simon wouldn't give up and kept going for a year.". Tears started rolling down Dave's cheeks now as if the tap had finally been turned on and the emotion could no longer be contained.

"When we first got the diagnosis, my family didn't know what to do. The doctors told us there was nothing we could do but wait for the end. We waited for the month to pass, but Simon was the only one of us that hadn't given up hope. He could still talk a bit back then, but he made me promise to him that I wouldn't give up hope and I would keep believing in him. He told me he wanted to try and make the rest of his life as normal as possible."

"My Mum and Dad didn't know what to say to that." Dave said, clearing his throat. "They agreed that they wanted to make him as comfortable as possible, but that the doctors told them he should stay at home and rest."

"But Simon was a cheeky git sometimes." Dave continued, "He wanted to go out and see the outside world. He wanted to keep experiencing the world whilst he still could."

"His strength gave me strength. It made me think of different ways that I could take him places and let him keep living his life. He had a basic wheelchair that worked ok for a few weeks, but soon it wasn't suitable for him anymore."

"My Mum and Dad went to the bank to borrow some money for a custom built wheelchair for him, but they didn't have any credit to get the kind of money needed. Before Simon stopped talking, he said to me to make one for him. So I did."

"I didn't know anything about electronics, but the best way of learning to do something is to just start doing it. So I did. I got parts from anywhere I could. The recycling center, peoples old electric appliances left outside for the council to take away, the scrap yard. When I did have some money I bought what I could off ebay, or charity shops, like where I got this crap suit from, to complete things. And after a week or so of fiddling and screwing and hammering it came together and it did its job. I could take him out to the cinema or to the park and get him out of the house again."

The waitress walked over to the table and set down the baguettes in front of them. Dave paused from his story for a bit and they both started eating their baguettes. Nigel wanted to hear more, but it was as if Dave realised he needed the strength the food would give him to continue his story. Nigel wondered when the last time Dave had eaten anything.

Once Dave had finished the first half of his baguette he looked back at Nigel and continued his story.

"Eventually, even I had to admit defeat with the new wheelchair. Simon started to need help to breathe and he couldn't leave the house anymore without the machines keeping him alive. This made me think. How could I make his last few months more than just sitting there waiting for his time to end? That's when I came up with the idea of the glasses."

"If we couldn't bring Simon outside, maybe we could bring the outside world to him. Let him experience life through the eyes of someone else. So I started researching what parts I would need and this led me to Amstaria, and then to you."

Nigel now understood Dave's reason for the project. Dave had told him it was all about making money and getting rich, but now he knew it was out of desperation to help his brother. He wanted to make a difference to his life.

"But it was all for nothing." said Dave disheartened, "I was too late. He didn't get a chance to use it. We were so close."

Dave put his head in his hands and burst into tears. Nigel didn't know what to say. He had never been in a situation like this before. He remembered what his Dad said, "Life doesn't have an instruction manual".

Nigel put his hand on Dave's shoulder before saying "Its so sad. I don't know what to say, but from what you have just told me about Simon, he wouldn't want you to give up. He would want you to keep going, keep on fighting."

Dave lifted his head out of his hands and looked at Nigel, his eyes even redder than before, but now with a glimmer of hope inside them.

"Nigel, you know, sometimes you say just the right thing." said Dave, "I might be too late for Simon, but we can still help others in his situation. Give them a chance to see the world."

Dave stood up and put his arms out. Dave stood up and they gave each other a hug, well, a man hug for a few seconds, patting each other on the back, before separating again.

"Do me a favour Nigel, won't you?" asked Dave.

"Sure thing. Anything." replied Nigel.

"Tell work I had a dodgy sandwich for lunch or something. I need to be with my family for a few days" Dave said.

"Sure, will do" Nigel promised.

Dave got up from his chair and put out his hand to Nigel, who shook his hand.

"See you in a few days mate" Nigel said, before turning and walking out of the cafe.

Nigel was still trying to understand everything he had just learnt about Dave. After knowing all that he didn't know how Dave managed to put on such a brave front all the time, but then knowing he was doing whatever he could to help his brother, it started to make sense. There is nothing stronger than a family bond.

HEADS UP

The time without Dave had given Nigel some time on his own to think. He wanted to keep working on the project whilst Dave was spending time with his family. He couldn't imagine what he was going through.

Nigel tried on the glasses with the screens and moved the other set with the camera around with his hand looking at the room. His first thought was that it looked real, but didn't look right for some reason. He fired up his laptop and did some quick searches for virtual reality. He soon realised the technology was good, but it was a long way from actual reality. He realised that people would expect it to be a bit more like a game and less real, otherwise they would feel something was wrong.

A lot of the virtual reality videos were for games and virtual worlds. The games had a certain style to them to make them unique to other games. Nigel remembered reading about digital filters for images and videos. There was a series of popular apps where you could take a photo and then run it through a filter to make it look like it was from the 1960's or like an old black and white photo. Nigel never really understood these apps as people were paying almost a thousand pound for a top of the range phone with a super high spec camera and then making the photo look old. Retro cool or something like that.

Nigel decided he would try and find a library where he could run the live video feed through to change it and give it a more gamified feel to it. He played around with a few different effects until he found the one he was after. It added a small outline to every shape it could identify, giving the video a subtle cartoon like effect.

The idea in Nigel's head was that if people thought it was the real world they would shy away and not explore and not talk to anyone. If it seemed like a really good virtual world then people would play it like a game and be more confident in what they were doing.

He thought about what people would want to do when they are using the system. To some people, simply experiencing walking around the town or looking out across a beautiful view like a sunset would be an amazing experience, but to others they would want more, especially if they are using it for a long time. Maybe they could add some challenges to it like try and discover a certain amount of items or talk to a certain number of people about certain subjects?

Also they would need to know the options of where they can go within the world they are viewing and how to get to a certain destination. They would need a sat nav. Nigel remembered using his phone to find the pub when he met up with Dave. That night seemed like such a long time ago but in reality was only a number of weeks. So much had changed since then.

Nigel searched for another library to add to his project that would allow him to add a sat nav style interface to the display. He would also need to speak to Dave about fitting a GPS receiver to the camera headset as Nigel didn't have a clue how to even begin with that side of it.

Nigel wasn't a designer but he knew where to find information about design and design tutorials. He read blog posts and watched videos until he had a basic understanding of what to do and what not to do. He started building a user interface that would overlay over the screens without being too intrusive.

Nigel tried on the headset to see the result of his work. The heads up display was born.

THE REUNION

Nigel had been keeping himself busy in the evenings tweaking his heads up display whilst he was waiting for Dave to return to work. At the beginning of the week he was happy with the work he was doing, but he just hoped that Dave would appreciate what he was doing. The last thing he wanted to do was step on Dave's toes.

They were partners in their project but the week going past without hearing from Dave had caused some of Nigel's old tendencies to come back. He felt his confidence was already lower than the beginning of the week without someone there supporting him or challenging him to do new things.

He had read about something called imposter syndrome and was wondering if he was being sucked into it. It was where people felt like imposters, like they had no right to be there, like they were going to be found out at any moment and exposed for the fraud they really were.

He had a dream that night that he was stood in front of a panel of four potential investors. They were asking him all sorts of technical questions about the device, which Nigel let Dave answer. Dave was back to his old self, full of confidence able to answer anything whilst maintaining his smile. One of the investors picked up the device and put it on. His first comment was "Did you get a 5 year old to make this heads up display? It completely ruins the product"

"Actually that was Nigel's contribution to the product." Dave replied.

Everyone turned to look at Nigel now, faces full of disappointment, even Dave's smile fading to a frown.

"It's designed to be easy to use and not to overwhelm the user..." Nigel started before he was quickly interrupted by another of the potential investors.

"Designed? I wouldn't go that far. Maybe cobbled together from a series of libraries" blurted the second investor.

The four investors and Dave started laughing before the second investor started talking again.

"I'm in, as long as your 'designer 'friend over there is cut out of the business. You need some proper staff that know what they are doing. This is business, you can't just keep stringing people along because they are your friends." the second investor finished.

"I'm in too, but on the same principle as my colleague here" said the first investor, before the other two investors nodded in agreement.

Nigel didn't know what to say. Was this some kind of joke or was this really happening? He turned to Dave for support. Dave smiled back at him briefly before the smile faded back to a serious looking face.

"They're right Nigel. You've got to go." Dave said, before walking over to the investors and shaking their hands.

An assistant stood up from the corner of the room and walked over to Nigel, indicating to him that he needed to leave the room. He started walking backwards slowly, step by step, but the distance seemed to extrapolate after each step, taking him further and further away from Dave and the investors with each step. The room started to get darker, but only in the corner Nigel was approaching, the rest of the room with the investors was as bright as day. The corner got darker and darker before fading out completely to black before Nigel woke from the dream with a start.

Nigel collected his thoughts, looked around his bedroom and realised it was a dream, but it felt so real. He thought to himself, once Dave has all the parts he needs he won't have any more need of Nigel and the convenient friendship would be over. With Dave's electronics genius he could hire anyone he wanted. He didn't need Nigel anymore. Nigel would be stuck back at his job at Amstaria, reading news articles about the next big thing and the incredible rise of Dave the CEO. There would be a footnote buried deep in a wikipedia page about Nigel being a co-founder, but ultimately, a temporary member of the organisation.

Nigel's alarm went off and he got himself ready for work and tried to comfort himself with one of his specialist coffees before leaving, but no matter how good the coffee was, the bad feelings just wouldn't go away.

Nigel got to work and sat down at his desk, getting himself for another day of reading, without anything fun to do or work on. He had finished setting up the intranet server and installing all the updates so it was now just running in the background doing its job. He wasn't really surprised the old Intranet manager left. The server basically looked after itself once it was set up.

Nigel loaded up his web browser and was thinking about what to read about today, when all of a sudden a message from the server chat service popped up on his screen.

"U alright m8?"

It was from Dave.

Nigel turned around to see Dave sat at his desk, looking over at Nigel. Dave gave Nigel a thumbs up along with a faint smile. Nigel understood. Dave was ok, not good, but doing ok, considering the circumstances.

"At urs tonite?" asked Dave.

Nigel wanted to jump up in the air and then run over and tell Dave all about what he had been working on and how he was so glad to see him and ask him all about his family and how they were doing, but that had to wait. He didn't know if Dave had told anyone else at work about his brother. For all they knew, his absence was from a dodgy sandwich at lunch last week, well, that's what Nigel said had happened anyway.

"Sure thing. Will be good to catch up." replied Nigel, keeping it controlled and concise.

The rest of the day seemed to pass a bit quicker than normal, but the last hour really dragged for some reason. Nigel walked home, tidied his table and then got project Victor out of the box and laid it on the table ready for Dave to come round later in the evening.

This time Dave knocked at the door whilst Nigel was still finishing his dinner. Nigel stood up, put his plate onto his chair and then went over and opened the door.

"Alright Nigel, how are you?" Dave asked.

"I'm great. It's good to see you Dave, how are you doing?" asked Nigel.

"Well, you know, it's been a tough week, but it's been nice to spend some time with the family. Lots of happy memories with Simon, both before and after the diagnosis. He was one in a million." Dave finished before taking a few seconds to compose himself after talking about his brother.

"Come on in. I've got some stuff to show you." Nigel said.

"Something to show me?" Dave said in a voice louder than it needed to be. "I ain't falling for that one again Nigel. You show me yours if I show you mine"

Nigel's neighbours looked through their windows at the sudden disturbance of Dave talking loudly, but Nigel didn't care. It was great to have the old Dave back for now, despite what the neighbours thought of him.

Nigel smiled at Dave before they both walked into the living room.

Before Nigel could explain what he had been working on over the past week, Dave picked up the glasses with the screens and put them on.

"What the?" Dave said. Nigel know it, he shouldn't have touched it whilst Dave was away.

"I was going to explain, you see I had this idea…" began Nigel.

"I love it!" said Dave "I hadn't thought about that effect with the video feed. It's like a game, but still feels real at the same time."

Dave told Nigel to put the other headset on so he could get the full effect.

"It's even got a heads up display now too!" Dave exclaimed.

"Yeah I thought it would make it more game like so people would be more confident playing and we could make challenges part of the game to make sure people explored new areas." Nigel said excitedly. "I almost forgot, I thought we could add GPS and make a sat nav style interface to help people know where they are going and help them get to a destination."

"Great idea Nigel. I love it. Where did you get the heads up display from?" Dave asked.

"Well, I started doing some research and it took a bit of trial and error but I think it worked out ok" Nigel replied.

"It's better than ok mate. It's the nuts!" complimented Dave.

Suddenly Nigel's dream from the previous night seemed like forever ago. It was amazing the difference a couple of complements made to his confidence. He no longer felt like an imposter, he felt like he belonged again.

"So what is the plan then?" asked Nigel, full of enthusiasm.

"Lets try it out in the real world" said Dave, taking the headset off and passing it to Nigel. "There you go. You go to the pub and I'll stay here and try it out."

"Are you sure it's ready?" Nigel questioned, suddenly feeling scared again. He wasn't sure what Dave would ask him to do out in the real world.

"There is only one way to find out how it will work. Don't worry, we'll take it steady for the first test." said Dave.

Nigel put on the glasses with the cameras, followed by the wrist sensors, then put his jacket over the top to hide the wires as best he could. As he was getting ready, Dave was putting on the headset.

"Comms check. Can you hear me?" Dave asked.

"Yep, loud and clear" replied Nigel. "Ok I guess I'll see you in a bit"

Nigel turned and walked out the house and into the street, closing his door behind him. He felt the cold of the evening hit him, but at least it was a dry night. He looked out across the street in both directions, trying to think which way was best to go to the pub. The last thing he wanted was to repeat his last journey to the pub with his sat nav shouting at him, followed by another trouser splitting moment.

"You alright?" he heard in his ears, waking him from his stupor. "Best to go left and along the High Street to the pub"

Nigel obeyed the instructions and turned to his left and headed towards the pub.

"It's a bit dark out. Maybe we could enhance the cameras with night vision or something." Dave said in Nigel's ear as Nigel walked past one of his neighbours taking out the rubbish.

"That's a good idea" he replied to Dave, but the neighbour heard Nigel talking and turned to look at Nigel, thinking he was speaking to him.

"What's that?" asked the neighbour.

"Umm, yeah, that's a good idea taking the rubbish out. I need to do mine when I get back home." Nigel improvised and walked off quickly.

"Ha. I guess you need to keep the talking to a minimum so people don't think you're crazy." said Dave.

Nigel just nodded in reply, afraid someone else would see him talking to himself.

Soon enough Nigel arrived at the pub and walked up to the bar. It was quite quiet in there tonight with only three customers, one other at the bar ordering a beer and a couple of others sat at a table, as well as Tracey the bar maid of course.

"Right, this should be fun. Remember to relax and try not to think about it too much, just follow the instructions and the arm movements as best you can. It will take a bit of practice to get just right." Nigel said. "Let's start with something simple"

"Walk over to Tracey and ask for a pint of lager"

Nigel waited for the other customer to finish paying for his drink and then ordered himself a pint. Tracey placed the pint on the bar and Nigel felt his wrist sensors moving. He concentrated on the movements to try and mimic them as best he could. He moved his right hand moved behind him, towards his back pocket and then paused for a second before moving it back. He looked at his empty hand then realised he was supposed to have taken his wallet out of his back pocket.

Dave made the movement again and Nigel followed again, this time getting his wallet out of his pocket to pay for the beer.

"That's it. Wanted to give you a little test rather than just shouting instructions in your ear."

Nigel looked around the pub, but no one was taking any notice of him. He opened his wallet and followed the movements to take a £10 note out and pass it to Tracey. She walked to the till and got Nigel's change. Nigel copied Dave's movements, turning his left hand over so it was palm up and outstretched ready for the change, before putting his hand in his pocket and dropping the change in it. Well, that was the plan anyway. The movements from the sensor were slightly missaligned and Dave ended up throwing most of the change on the floor.

Nigel bent down and hurriedly picked the change up, before putting it back in his pocket.

"Another one for the bugs list there Nigel." said Dave.

"You alright love?" asked Tracey, seeing Nigel's slightly panicked look on his face.

"All the better for seeing you Tracey" said Dave instinctively, before Nigel repeated it out loud.

"Didn't know you knew my name" said Tracey. "Can't remember seeing you in here before."

Nigel felt relieved his leather trouser and squelching shoes evening wasn't still fresh in her memory.

"Oh yeah, I recognise you. Aren't you mates with Dave?" Tracey asked.

So maybe she did remember him after all, but was just being polite not mentioning his get up from the previous outing. Nigel thought to himself that Tracey had probably seen a lot worse that

that in her time working at the pub. Maybe it was just a minor incident in her work experience.

"Yes, Dave is a good mate of mine" said Dave, Nigel repeating it.

"Say hi to him from me when you see him won't you. He's a nice guy, always friendly" replied Tracey.

"Ohh yes, you hear that Nigel!" said Dave excitedly. "Stop, don't say that!" Dave quickly explained.

"Ooh yes" said Nigel, before the rest of the message came through the ear piece, stopping him.

"Umm, yes I will" Nigel corrected himself.

The bar maid smiled and turned to another customer, one from the table this time.

"Sorry about that Nigel. Got a bit carried away. She's a beaut isn't she" Dave said, his non existent chances of going out with Tracey suddenly taking a sharp rise. Nigel nodded, not wanting to look crazy in front of the people in the pub.

Nigel took a quick look at the customer at the bar next to him. He was 6 foot 4, with huge muscles, shaved head and a long leather jacket. He didn't want to upset this guy if he could avoid it.

"Now let's try taking a sip of beer. Remember to try and copy the movements as best you can."

Nigel took a deep breath and tried to concentrate on the task and not the large man making his order next to him. He followed the movements and stretched out his right arm towards the pint on the bar. He grasped the pint and then followed the movements back towards his face and started tipping the glass.

There must of been a slightly different sense of perspective from what Dave could see compared to Nigel in the real world. The pint glass was not quite close enough to Nigel's mouth and beer started to dribble over the top of the glass towards Nigel. He instinctively moved his head forward to try and catch the dribbling liquid in his mouth, but he wasn't quite ready for it and ended up knocking the glass slightly with his lips, sending a few mouthfuls of beer towards the large customer and his long leather jacket.

The splat sound was pretty loud in the quiet pub.

The tall man heard it and turned to look down at the newly acquired beer stains on his leather jacket. He turned to look at Nigel with a serious looking frown upon his face. He clenched his fists in front of him, ready to strike.

"Ok Nigel, follow my lead" said Dave.

"But.. I... ummm..." Nigel didn't know what to say or do. Out of sheer panic he started following the arm movements from the sensors, feeling his right hand move back behind his right shoulder, before swinging quickly towards the tall man's stomach, landing a powerful blow.

The man crumpled at the surprisingly efficient punch.

"Right now run for it!" shouted Dave.

Nigel didn't need to be told twice. He legged it out of the pub as quickly as he could, seeing the second man from the table get up to help his winded mate in the mirror before he got out the door.
Nigel ran for as long as he could before he stopped, panting and bending over with his hands on his knees, trying to get his breath back.

"I've never hit anyone before" Nigel said between deep breaths, sucking in air into his lungs.

"You couldn't tell from that punch! It could have been a finishing move from Mortal Kombat" Dave laughed. "Well, it's not the kind of test that I thought we would be doing tonight, but as a combat simulator it ticks all the boxes. He went down like a sack of spuds!"

"You keep laughing, you were safely back indoors whilst I was the one on the front line" said Nigel, his breathing starting to slow after the adrenaline rush started to subside. "I'm coming home now. I think that's enough for one night"

"Yeah, I'd say that's a pretty successful first attempt in the real world" said Dave. "We have lots of info to go through and a few alignment bugs to sort out before next time!"

"Alignment bugs, that's one way of putting it." replied Nigel.

He took a long deep breath in before slowly breathing it out again, trying to regain control. He walked the rest of the way home, trying to subdue the buzz that came from his first ever bar fight.

When he got there, he took all of the headset and wires off and placed them on the table. Dave had already taken his headset off.

"It's lucky he didn't get a punch in to your face, he could have set us back weeks of development time smashing up those glasses" Dave laughed.

"Thanks for your concern over my personal safety" Nigel replied, smiling back.

"Well, it's been an eventful evening. I think I had better get off home." Dave said. "By the way, I hooked up a recorder to the live video feed if you want to watch your sucker punch back. Oh and don't miss listening to the panicky squealing noises you made as you ran for you life."

"Cheers Dave!" said Nigel.

Dave slowly stood up, shook Nigel's hand and made his way home.

Nigel sat down on his sofa, his head spinning from the events of the evening. At least he had something to talk about with his parents when he made his weekly catch up call, although he may miss out some of the details. He didn't want his Mum getting upset and forcing his Dad to drive them all the way to his house so she could make sure he was alright. Thinking about it, it may be best not to recite the evenings events to his parents after all.

THE BIG BOSS

The next morning, Shiny Shoes sat in his office and opened up his emails. He started skimming through them, picking important looking ones to read and others to file away in the recycle bin, when one came to his attention. The email was flagged as VIP, a very rare email from the director based at the head office.

"Oh god, what do they want now?" Shiny Shoes thought to himself. He liked to keep a well run department, meeting sales targets, but not exceeding them, keeping things smooth and consistent. If there was a large sale that would take them too far over the target he would do a bit of creative accounting and put the invoice date back a few days to help out in the next sales target. That meant head office normally left him well alone, but not today.

He opened the email and started reading.

"Dear Sir,

We have identified that you have ordered prototype cameras under the purposes of demo stock. As these devices are valued highly we would like to know the potential sales volume you will be forecasting as a result of the demo stock delivery.

We are very much looking forward to seeing your improved sales targets for the coming months.

Many thanks,

Kimberly McDoble
Head Office"

"Prototype cameras? What the hell is this? I haven't requested any prototype cameras" Shiny Shoes said out loud to himself. He considered deleting the email, assuming it was sent in error, but thought better of it as, after all, it was from the big boss.

He went to the corner of his office and pulled out a box of order forms, all hand written by the sales staff and manually signed by him. He went through the order forms one by one checking for any prototype cameras that might have been ordered by mistake or any writing that may have smudged before the order forms were faxed over to the head office.

It took him over an hour to go through the whole box of orders but none of them looked suspicious or mentioned prototype cameras. All had his own signature on them, not trusting any of the office workers to make their own orders.

He went back to his computer and clicked reply on the email and started typing.

"Hello Kimbery,
Many thanks for your email. I have been through all of our order forms that we have sent over to you in the past two months and none contain any orders for prototype cameras.

I can only assume this email was sent in error.

Many thanks,"

He signed it with his name and pressed send. "Right, thats that dealt with", he thought to himself and went on reading through the rest of his emails.

In Head Office, Kimberly opened the reply and started reading, not impressed with what she was reading. She picked up her telephone and dialled her assistant, asking her to make travel arrangements to go and pay this office a visit to discuss matters face to face.

THE AUDIT

The next day, Nigel was sat at his desk, looking at the direction of his screen, but not actually paying attention to anything on the screen. He was lost in thought, thinking about the design of a website to launch their project to the world. What domain name should they use? They would have to check what names are available before they get too far into their marketing campaign.

Nigel had read about start up companies thinking they owned a particular domain name and spending thousands on advertising and printing flyers, only to realise that they never actually got round to buying the domain name. In the meantime, a cyber squatter had got their first and bought the domain name for £9.99 but would sell it to the company for a "very reasonable" admin fee of £10,000.

The office was generally quite relaxed today, being the Friday before the weekend started. The sales people had mostly met their targets for the week so were making a few chase up calls to keep themselves busy, but in no rush to close the deal. People were taking more coffee breaks than normal and each coffee break would last a little bit longer each time with the discussions going from a friendly hello, into a lengthy discussion about weekend plans.

A large executive car pulled into the car park and Kimberly

stepped out.

The receptionist saw the car pull up and as Kimberly was stepping out of the car, the receptionist hung up the call she was on and immediatley dialled Shiny Shoes.

"Hello, how can I hel…" started Shiny Shoes.

"CODE RED! CODE RED!" the receptionist cut him off and shouted her warning before hanging up as quickly as she has picked up the phone.

Shiny Shoes had told the receptionist to use the code red protocol if an executive was to turn up, but it had never actually happened before. He thought it would be a good way to keep the receptionists attentive, rather than sat there talking to other members of staff or talking to their friends on the phone when no one was listening.

Upstairs, Shiny Shoes jumped up from his desk in a panic. He ran out of his office as fast as he could and shouted "Look busy!" at the staff, before running back into his office and sitting back into his chair and tidying any loose papers on his desk.

The staff at the coffee machine stopped their discussions and went back to their desks, whether they had added milk and sugar to their coffee or not.

The phone switchboard suddenly lit up as the sales people found any lead they could possibly chase up to try and look busy.

The sudden buzz disturbed Nigel from his thoughts of his website design. He didn't know what was going on but he saw the coffee machine was finally free so he got up and walked over to the kitchen to make himself a coffee.

Dave saw Nigel getting up and started writing a message to Nigel to tell him to stay at his desk, but he couldn't type fast enough and Nigel had already left his desk before the message was sent.

Nigel was making himself a coffee, taking his time as it wasn't like he had much work to do and if it was worth making a coffee, it was worth doing it properly.

Kimberly walked up the stairs and into the office. Shiny Shoes saw her and expected her to walk directly into his office. He picked up the phone, without dialling it, to pretend he was in the middle of an important phone call when she entered, except she didn't enter his office. Instead she walked past and kept going.

Kimberly smelt the coffee from the coffee machine and decided she wanted a fresh cup for herself after her long drive. She hadn't smelt coffee that good for a long time. It was not the standard, cheap, tasteless coffee that all the other offices used. Kimberly entered the staff kitchen and saw Nigel at the machine.

"Hello, I'm Kimberly" she said, introducing herself to Nigel. Most staff in the other offices knew Kimberly by sight, or they knew the name Kimberly. She was the kind of person that everyone talked about by first name only, knowing when people talked about Kimberly, they were talking about THE Kimberly.

Nigel looked up, wondering who was interrupting his concentration for his perfect cup of coffee. He didn't recognise the lady stood in the doorway and even though he had spent many hours in the office reading from the internet, the one site he had never bothered looking at was the Amstaria corporate website. He didn't respond immediately, instead he looked back at his coffee for a couple of seconds and then shut off the machine to finish making his coffee.

"Hello, I'm Nigel" he eventually replied, before walking around the machine, extending his hand for a handshake.

Kimberly extended her hand and shook it firmly. She was impressed with this guy. Normally when she entered a room and introduced herself she the person in the room would be so nervous they would start shaking and stuttering, or even just stand there in silence, afraid they might say something wrong, so just said nothing.

"That coffee smells good" Kimberly said, smiling to Nigel. "You look like you know how to work that machine, I'll have a cappuccino, skimmed milk and no sugar."

Nigel looked at her, wondering why she couldn't make herself a coffee. Why should he waste his skills making a coffee for this newby. He thought to himself she was probably just another new sales person, but he didn't want to be rude to someone he had just met.

"Tell you what, I can show you how to make a coffee if you want" Nigel replied. "That way, you can make yourself one later on if you want another one."

Kimberly was taken aback again. Normally people just smiled and nodded at her when she asked for a coffee. She was intrigued by Nigel. Maybe he didn't know who she was or maybe he was just super confident. She walked over to the machine and stood next to Nigel.

When she was next to Nigel, he took it as a sign to begin the instructions.

"Right, the first thing to do is to grind the coffee. Great coffee starts with freshly ground coffee" Nigel began.

Shiny Shoes was in a real panic now, wondering why the hell Kimberly was talking to Nigel of all people. He got up from his desk and hurried over to the kitchen to interrupt the conversation as quickly as he could before Nigel said something stupid that would make him look bad.

"Next you need to warm the coffee cup before filling it with coff.." Nigel started

"Kimberly! What a wonderful surprise to see you. I'm..." Shiny Shoes interrupted Nigel, but was himself interrupted, but not by anything anyone said, simply by a glare from Kimberly.

Kimberly paused for a few seconds, before talking.

"Hello. I will speak to you once I have finished here" Kimberly said in a calm and precise manner.

Shiny Shoes didn't know what to say so he just nodded extremely fast with his mouth a gape. He backed out of the kitchen and walked slowly back to his office, now a gibbering wreck.

Nigel didn't know what the hell just happened, but he continued his instructions, showing Kimberly how to make a cup of coffee. Once he had finished, he handed her the coffee and smiled.

"Enjoy" Nigel said, and with that he turned and walked out of the kitchen, carrying his own coffee, and went back to his desk to continue his thought stream.

Kimberly put the fresh coffee to her lips and took a sip. It had to be the best coffee she had ever tasted. She didn't know what Nigel did there, but if they ever had to shut this office down, there was one employee she would like to relocate to head office, even if it was just to make her coffee.

Kimberly stood in the kitchen and finished her coffee. It was her usual tactic to keep people waiting, to let them stew a bit more before going to talk to them, to let them know who is in control of the situation, but this time it was more to enjoy every last drop of the coffee in her cup. Making Shiny Shoes wait was just an added bonus.

Once she had finished she put her coffee cup down and walked to Shiny Shoes office. Luckily by now he had regained some of his composure and was able to hold a fairly coherent conversation.

Shiny Shoes stood up and held his hand out for a handshake "Hello Kimberly, how nice to see you. How may I help you today?" Kimberly didn't say anything and didn't extend the courtesy of a handshake to him. Shiny Shoes pulled his hand back to his side before gesturing to the chair on the other side of his desk. "Please take a seat."

Kimberly sat down in the chair opposite the desk and Shiny Shoes sat down in his own chair behind the desk.

"From your response yesterday, I can only conclude that you do not know how to run your office, allowing your staff to order whatever parts they feel like ordering." Kimberly said, getting straight to the point. "Your office is in receipt of a prototype camera and you have until the end of next week to locate it, or instead of looking for a camera you will be looking through the job adverts."

Shiny Shoes didn't argue. He had lost this conversation before it had even started.

Kimberly stood up, followed quickly by Shiny Shoes, once more outstretching his hand for a handshake, but he was again left hanging as Kimberly turned and left his office. She walked directly to the door to reception, but as she opened the door, she glanced into Shiny Shoes office, seeing him sat at his desk with his head in his hands. She then glanced over her shoulder and took a quick look at Nigel, with him sat there as if it was any normal day. There was something different about him, she thought to herself, before continuing into reception and back into the executive car that was sat waiting for her.

The car pulled away and headed back to head office, Kimberly's work done, for this week at least.

It took Shiny Shoes at least an hour before he managed to get himself under control enough to leave his office. He stood just outside the doorway and coughed loudly to get everyone's attention.

"Right! It has come to my attention that someone has been placing orders without my permission. This is not the way I run this office!" Shiny Shoes shouted. "I expect the person who has ordered a prototype camera to return it in pristine condition on my desk before 9am on Monday morning, along with their resignation."

The office staff looked around at each other, not knowing where to look. Dave and Nigel tried desperately not to look at each other, knowing it was them that had placed the order to build their project, not wanting to show any signs of guilt.

"Any questions?" Shiny Shoes continued. "No? Good"

Shiny Shoes then turned and walked back into his office, slamming the door shut behind him to make sure people felt the impact of what he had just said.

Nigel sank in his chair. What had he done. He had only known Dave for a short period of time, but things had changed so much for him. He had taken too many risks and was now paying the price. Who would want to hire someone after they had been fired? Who would want to hire someone without any chance of getting a reference.

All the confidence and excitement from the experiences Nigel had had over the past few weeks had been washed away in an instant. He could feel himself reverting to the super shy and quiet person he had once been before he met Dave.

The rest of the day passed in a blur, with Nigel convinced there was no way out from this situation. This would be his last day working for Amstaria. He was sure of it.

THE AFTERMATH

Nigel looked down at the ground as he walked slowly home, unaware that Dave was walking behind him. After they were a safe distance from work and sure there was no one else within earshot, Dave walked up to Nigel and tapped him on the shoulder.

"Alright mate. That was a close one earlier wasn't it" Dave laughed, but Nigel was not impressed.

"Everything is a joke to you isn't it?" Nigel said as he turned to look Dave in the eye. "I can't believe I've been so stupid, ordering those parts and taking them from work!"

"We're just borrowing them for a bit. They weren't using them" Dave continued to smile, convinced he could use his charm one more time on Nigel.

"It isn't borrowing Dave, it's stealing!" Nigel said, getting right in Dave's face. "There, I've said it. Now leave me alone."

"Hold up, hold up. We can sort this out. They don't know who did it do they, otherwise they would have been straight on to us" Dave said. "You know, silver lining and all that"

This time Dave's charm was not working. Nigel was getting more angry by the second.

"You are full of it. I can't believe you still think everything is ok."

Nigel shouted back to Dave. "I'm getting fired on Monday and that's the end of the story. No silver linings, no clever way out. That's it. End of my career."

Nigel felt a rage building inside him. He clenched his fists up tight, but he still had control. He looked at Dave and couldn't help thinking of Dave's brother Simon. He realised now how desperate Dave really was to succeed, not wanting to stop for anything in his way as he knew he didn't have much time left. But Nigel couldn't forgive Dave for dragging him down with him.

Nigel shook his head, regaining his composure.

"Please, just leave me alone" Nigel said, before turning away and walking back to his house.

This time, Dave didn't follow him.

FIGHTING BACK

Nigel didn't sleep very well that night for obvious reasons. He decided to give up trying to sleep about 4am and went downstairs and made himself a cup of coffee. He took the coffee into his living room, sat in his chair and got his laptop out. He started writing his resume, in the vain attempt of looking for a new job before he lost his on Monday. He wrote out his education and his qualifications, before writing his work experience.

He wrote down the year and month he had started with Amstaria.

He looked at the date he had written down. How had he been there for so long and achieved absolutely nothing with his career. He was so full of aspirations when he started, but they were quickly washed away with no mentor and no prospects. He just grew comfortable and safe.

He wished he was still in that safe and comfortable place right now, instead of hours away from being fired.

He started to write his job title "Intranet Manager" but then couldn't put his job description into words as it didn't really exist. He thought about what he could write and began typing: "Responsible for the office intranet, but I didn't actually get the server out of the box for years.".

Maybe not.

Nigel deleted the section and began to write again: "Responsible for Intranet Server, with no outages in the many years I was in charge of it, mainly due to the fact I didn't plug it in."

He gave up on the job description for now and decided to write some references instead. He wrote his university tutor's contact details, not knowing if she was still working at the university or not.

The only other reference he could put was Amstaria. He wasn't sure it was even worth putting it down in the current circumstances, but thought it would raise more questions why he hasn't put his current employer down as a reference than not putting it down.

Nigel started writing the HR department's contact details but then realised he didn't know the address. He opened his browser and started searching for Amstaria HR department. He found the link to the head office website and clicked on the link. He started scrolling down to the contact details in the footer, but a name caught his eye, so he scrolled back up to read the section.

The name on the webpage was Kimberly.

How strange, he thought to himself, seeing the same name as the person he met in the office the other day. He was about to scroll back down to the footer, but instead, began reading the section about Kimberly, soon realising this Kimberly was the CEO for the UK. He thought this is obviously just a coincidence and could not be the same person he met.

Until he scrolled a little further down and saw a picture of her, before giving himself the mother of all facepalms.

"What did you do at work today" Nigel said to himself. "Oh not much, just taught the CEO how to make a cup of coffee."

Nigel put his laptop down on the table, resisting the urge to smash it into a thousand pieces only by thinking he might need the cash he could sell it for in the near future. He got up and went back to bed and stayed there most of the day.

When Nigel got the courage to get out of bed once more he went downstairs and sat in his chair. As he did so he knocked the laptop, stirring it to life. He reached over to turn the laptop off, not wanting to see any more about Amstaria ever again, but as he looked at the screen there was a quote from Kimberly.

"I want to lead Amstaria into the next decade through cutting edge technology and innovation"

He looked from his laptop, to the box where their device was located, and back to the laptop, reading the quote once more.

He stood up and ran upstairs to get dressed as quickly as he could, before grabbing the box and his laptop, heading for the train station.

THE DEMO

Nigel bought the first train ticket he could that would get him as close to the Amstaria head office as he could. He got on the train and opened up the laptop. He found Kimberly's last name from the Amstaria company website and searched for her address, but to no avail.

Instead he found an article written in a magazine about women in tech firms which showed a picture of her outside her £4 million house. The name of the house was written in large brass letters arching over the top of the black painted gates. Knowing the house name made it much easy to find by doing a quick search on a mapping website. He planned the route from the train station to her house so he could tell the taxi driver where to go, once he had reached the station.

It was a long journey so Nigel used the time to prepare the equipment and do as much research as he could.

Once the train reached the station he ran out of the carriage carrying his laptop and box and then jumped in a taxi heading straight for the house.

When he got to the large black gates, he climbed out of the taxi with his belongings and paid the taxi driver. The driver asked if he should wait and Nigel replied "No it's ok." before the taxi driver just shrugged and drove off.

Nigel suddenly realised that it was now 10pm at night and he was stood outside the gates of a £4 million pound house with no jacket, and just a laptop and a box. Maybe he should have thought this through a bit more. What was he thinking, he could just ring the buzzer and walk right in, that she would let any crazy looking person into her house at this time of night.

He was about to turn around and run after the taxi to get it to take him home, but then he thought about Dave and what would he do. He imagined that it was the other night with Dave in control of him, giving him instructions through his ear piece and controlling his arms through the sensors. He would do what Dave would do, convincing himself that he needed to act strong and not become his former reclusive self.

This was his chance and he was going to take it.

He walked to the gates and pressed the buzzer. A small screen came on and he saw Kimberly looking at him.

"Yes, can I help you?" she said

"Hello, you might not remember me but I need 10 minutes of your time, its urgent." Nigel replied

"You do know it's 10pm don't you?" she questioned

"Yes, but this can't wait until tomorrow. You need to see it now" asserted Nigel. He would not take no for an answer.

"Hang on a minute, I know you from somewhere don't I?" she said "Cappuccino guy?"

She looked confused, as would most people be, when a guy she met at work was stood outside the gates to her house at this time of night carrying a laptop and a box. She always had a knack for spotting people with that extra something. She knew they shouldn't, but first impressions always mattered a lot to her. She knew instantly what people were like by the way they reacted to her and she had felt like this man stood at her gates had something special about him when they met yesterday.

"I don't normally do this, but I'm buzzing you in" she said to Nigel "Just don't make me regret my decision"

"Absolutely. See you in a minute" Nigel said, as the gates clicked open and he started walking down the driveway to the house. It was at this point he looked down along the driveway and realised how long the driveway actually was. Maybe he should have kept that taxi around afterall.

In the distance, at the end of the driveway, he could see an imposing stone built mansion house. The house was lit up from the outside to demonstrate the grandeur to visitors no matter what time of day it was. Along the long walk, Nigel started to count the number of windows and guess the number of rooms, before shaking his head trying to clear the intimidating thoughts that had just entered his head, trying to focus on the task at hand.

When he got to the large, imposing front door, he knocked twice and it was opened by a maid. She looked Nigel up and down, even more confused as to why her boss Kimberly had let him in than before she had seen him.

"Miss McDoble has asked if you could meet her in the study. She will be along shortly" said the maid.

Nigel followed the maid into the house, looking around at the huge hallway and the grand staircase trying to take it all in, before he realised the maid was already quite a few steps ahead of him. He walked quickly to catch up with the maid so he didn't get lost. They left the hallway and entered a large room with books lining the walls and a large wooden desk in the centre. The desk had two chairs, one either side.

The maid pointed to the chair nearest the door, indicating Nigel to sit and wait there. Nigel sat down in the chair and the maid turned and left out of the door they had entered through. Nigel looked around the room, reading some of the book titles, wondering if anyone had ever read these books or if they were there purely for decoration. It looked like the kind of place where there would be a hidden passageway that operated by pulling the right book out of the shelf.

He looked at the belongings he had brought with him and then started arranging his box or equipment and laptop on the desk and waited for Kimberly.

Unlike Shiny Shoes, she didn't keep him waiting for long, she already had to wait ten minutes for Nigel to walk down the driveway. She was curious to find out what the fuss was all about. She walked into the study wearing a smart professional looking outfit, with the exception of slippers on her feet. Nigel wondered if she ever stopped working.

"So we meet again." Kimberly started, holding her hand out towards Nigel, who stood and shook her hand "It's funny, I had a feeling I would see you again, just not this quickly"

"Thank you for your time." Nigel said, but he didn't want to waste anymore time, he wanted to get straight to it. "I appreciate this is not the usual way of conducting business, but I have some things I need to tell you."

"Go on" said Kimberly, appreciating the fact Nigel didn't try and spend 10 minutes of her time trying to make small talk. They sat down on either side of the desk.

"It was me who ordered the prototype camera, but for a very good reason." Nigel took a deep breath before continuing. "I met someone who has turned my life upside down and is driven to succeed no matter what. I believed in him and I think you should too. He is a genius with electronics and his motives are for a really good cause."

Nigel looked at Kimberly for a few seconds to try and gauge her opinion of him, but she was using her world class poker face right now, giving nothing away. The face she had used in many boardroom meetings in the past with other men who would try and charm her into signing a contract or agreeing a sale. This was not her first time getting a pitch, although it was the first time she had someone buzz her house gate at 10pm.

"Before I show you this idea I need you to make me a promise." Nigel said, but seeing no response from Kimberly. "I need you to promise that Dave will be given the copyright to the design and that 50% of profits from private sales will be given to a foundation to help support people in the same situation as Dave's late brother."

Kimberly's poker face broke into a smile. She wasn't used to demands such as these. Normal contract negotiations were more like people offering anything and everything to get her to sign the deal, offering massive discounts to get her to agree to the deal.

"These are quite high demands indeed." she said, but the demands only made her more intrigued to find out what he had to offer. "Very well, I agree. Please continue"

Nigel wanted to make sure she really did agree before continuing.

"This may sound silly, but could you just say 'I agree, Dave owns the copyright 'for me?" asked Nigel. He looked at Kimberly and saw a quick flash as she started to roll her eyes, before she caught herself and the smile returned to her face.

"Ok. I agree, Dave owns the copyright" said Kimberly.

Nigel heard a voice in his head telling him to act calm and carry on. He imagined it was Dave telling him through an earpiece but in fact it was his own inner voice becoming stronger.

"Great. What Dave has designed is a solution to enable people to experience the real world in a way they would never get the chance to in real life. There is no better way of explaining this than a demonstration"

Nigel opened the box and removed the headsets. First, he gave the headset with the screens to Kimberly, before placing the headset with the camera on himself. He helped her get the motion sensors on her wrists, before putting his own on.

"As you can see, you can see everything I can see. And when you move your arms, my arms will move too."

As she moved her arms, he mimicked the movement using the feedback from the wrist straps.

"So the idea is, someone can wear the equipment I am wearing and go and do something that the rest of us take for granted, like walking down the beach or seeing the sunset, or something more extreme like climbing a mountain, and the person wearing the equipment you are wearing can experience it first hand."

He took the glasses off and looked at Kimberly. She removed the headset and looked back at him.

"I understand your intentions with this and I appreciate your honesty about why you ordered those parts. It's a difficult world we live in and some of us want to make the best of it for others." she replied, looking at Nigel. "There is something special about you. I noticed it when we first met. Most people shy away from me once they realise who I am, but instead you came all this way to see me."

Kimberly stood and paced back and forth along the edge of the large desk. Not saying anything, but deep in thought. After a moment, she stopped and looked at Nigel.

Nigel's heart was in his mouth. He didn't know what was going to happen next. He hadn't thought that far ahead. He had acted on impulse, not planning his sales pitch, not planning what he was going to wear and say, he just did it because he knew that he might never get this chance again. He didn't let the fear of not succeeding get in his way, all he had to do was try and that would be enough.

He was impressed that he got this far and that he had managed to show the demo, but Kimberly's poker face was back and she was gazing into his eyes, reading his emotions like an open book. He held his breath waiting for her response.

As her eyes gazed at him he expected her to say no, he expected her to throw him out of her house and then phone the police to get him arrested for stealing, but instead, she said "Yes".

Nigel stood still for a second whilst his brain processed what she had said, before running it through his head again one more time to make sure. Once he had convinced himself he jumped up in the air and cheered out loud. He had done it.

"Great. Let's meet again next week. I'll come to your office on Monday and we can sort out the paperwork. I can't wait to meet Dave as well." Kimberly said.

Nigel was smiling from ear to ear.

"One last question for this evening, do you need a lift home?" she asked.

"Oh that's very kind of you but it's a bit of a long drive for you?" said Nigel.

Kimberly laughed, "I meant my driver will take you home, I need to catch up on my beauty sleep"

"Of course, yes please" replied Nigel.

Kimberly put out her hand and Nigel shook it.

"A pleasure doing business with you." Kimberly smiled and walked out of the study.

Nigel couldn't believe what was going on. He was still smiling like a mad man when the driver came in 10 minutes later. Nigel quickly put all of his equipment away in the box and grabbed his laptop. The driver signalled to Nigel to follow him and they walked to the car waiting out the front of the house. Nigel got into the back and the driver shut the door behind him.

The driver drove Nigel all the way back to his house. Nigel couldn't wait to tell Dave all about it tomorrow, but first he needed to get some sleep.

THE NEGOTIATION

Nigel walked into the office on Monday morning with a new sense of confidence and swagger. He went and made himself a coffee and sat at his desk, unable to concentrate on any real work, feeling too excited for his meeting with Kimberly.

He had gotten in to work earlier than usual as he had one more thing he wanted to prepare before the meeting later that day.

Dave walked into the office just before 9am and saw Nigel sat at his desk. Nigel nodded to him and Dave nodded back in recognition but didn't look happy. Dave sat down at his desk.

Nigel opened his chat program and started a chat with Dave.

"Don't be mad, sorry about what I said on Friday. I need to talk to you, you see I took an opportunity at the weekend" Nigel typed.

"Glad ur talking to me again." Dave typed back, before adding "Who's the lucky lady then?"

"Ha ha, no, I mean about our work." Nigel replied, "I took a chance and told someone very influential about our project. Long story short, it worked out and we are getting a contract."

"Wot, rlly?" Dave asked, unsure how Nigel could have pulled off such a turnaround in a couple of days.

"You know that Kimberly that was here on Friday, well, I went to see her and talked to her. I gave her a demo and she was very impressed." Nigel typed.

"No way!" Dave replied "I new u could do it Nigel!"

Nigel thought back to what they had been through since they had met and how Dave's belief in him had changed his life. He had taken a chance, a chance that he would have never of even considered taking before they met.

"We are going to have a meeting today to go through the details, but Kimberly said you would keep all the copyright for the design and we'd create a foundation for charity." Nigel typed, smiling to himself.

"Fantastic!" Dave replied, as the office door opened and Kimberly walked in, but this time she was not on her own, she had a couple of other people with her in expensive looking suits. She walked directly to the meeting room with the other two people.

Shiny Shoes saw her walk past his office again and immediately rose to his feet to talk to her.

"Hello Kimberly, I wasn't expecting you back so soon..." Shiny Shoes began.

"Miss McDoble has a prearranged meeting and is not to be disturbed" said one of the people in the suits, cutting Shiny Shoes off.

Shiny Shoes stopped talking and nodded in acceptance, before walking back to his office, in a panic once more, wondering what was going on.

Nigel saw one of the suits get up and close the door to the meeting room, before sitting down at the table with the other suit and Kimberly. They began an important looking discussion, but Nigel could only guess what it was about as the meeting room had pretty good double glazing to keep the sound in the room. The suit who didn't close the door opened a briefcase and placed two stacks of paper onto the table next to two empty chairs.

After about ten minutes, the suit who closed the door opened it again and walked towards Nigel.

"Hello there Nigel. Please can we have ten minutes of your time?" he said to Nigel. Nigel got up and followed the suit, as he walked over to Dave and asked the same to him. Dave got up and followed the two of them back to the meeting room, before the suit closed the door behind them.

They all sat down at the table in the meeting room, Dave and Nigel taking the chairs with the stacks of paper in front of them.

"Hello again Nigel" said Kimberly smiling, as she stretched out her hand for a handshake, with Nigel reaching back and shaking her hand in return. "And this must be Dave" she continued, before shaking hands with Dave as well.

"Ok, let's begin shall we" Kimberly said. Her smile quickly disappeared from her face and the mood in the meeting room suddenly turned serious.

"Last week I was made aware that a prototype camera was ordered and delivered to this office and was presumed missing. It has since come to my attention that it had been taken and used in a non work related project. This is against company policy and as such against your employment terms and conditions, and as such, gross misconduct, leading to dismissal"

To summarise, this was not what Nigel had expected.

"In front of you are two contracts that state you acknowledge your wrong doing and that you will return any equipment taken from your place of work along with any related equipment and or software. You will then be escorted from the building and one months salary will be paid into your bank account, terminating your employment with immediate effect."

Nigel looked at Dave, but Dave didn't look back at Nigel. Dave was pissed. His usual calm and jokey exterior was gone, realising everything he had worked on was going to be taken away from him and Nigel.

"You can't do this, it's not right!" Dave stood and shouted at the other three.

The other three sat calmly and smugly, knowing they had the trump cards.

Dave sat down. The fight had gone from him. He hated these kind of people. All they cared about was making themselves richer. They didn't care about anyone's personal circumstances or what was right. They went straight for the jugular, chewed you up and spat you out. Dave knew they couldn't mount any type of legal battle against this.

Nigel didn't like seeing Dave like this. The only other time he had seen him like this was the day after his brother had died.

But Nigel was strangely calm. He knew something that no one else in the room knew.

"Kimberly, when I spoke to you at the weekend, this is not what we discussed. You agreed that Dave would own the copyright. Where has all this come from?" Nigel asked.

"I have no idea what you are talking about." said Kimberly, through her smug, perfect smile. "I would never agree to such a thing"

"Well you did. How can you go back on your word?" Nigel pleaded, sounding a bit more desperate now.

"A little lesson for you in future Nigel, get something written down, recorded, like these contracts you have in front of you. Now sign and get out of my building" Kimberly said, accidently letting her enjoyment slip out a bit too much.

Dave picked up the pen and removed the lid about to start signing the contract. He couldn't wait to get out of there.

Just before Dave put the pen to the paper, Nigel reached out and pulled the pen away. Dave looked at Nigel, confused.

"So I should have gotten something recorded when I spoke to you?" Nigel asked.

"That's what I said, now sign the paper!" Kimberly said as she pointed to the contract in front of Nigel.

"Before I sign, can I tell you a little story?" asked Nigel.
"Sure, just make it quick" replied Kimberly, losing her patience.

"I don't know if you are into video games, you don't really seem like the type of people that play games to me, but gaming is now a bigger industry than films. The strange thing is, that some people don't even play the game themselves, they like to spend their time watching other people play games. There are huge online streaming sites where people upload their live feeds of them playing a computer game."

"Lovely story, but what's the point?" Kimberly snapped back.

"Well, the point is, whilst I was on the train I had an idea. I thought it would be a good enhancement to allow live streaming from the device so other people could see what was going on. I also thought it would be a good enhancement to record and then playback your game later, you know, if something you didn't expect happened so you could try something different the next time."

"Or, for instance if someone said one thing and then decided to change their mind later, you would have, ohh, what word am I looking for, ah yes, recorded evidence. Like, for example a recording stating that Dave is the owner of the copyright."

The smug smile suddenly faded from Kimberly's face, she looked across to the two suits frantically, hoping they would be able to give her a way out of the situation unfolding in front of her.

"You see, the internet is a place full of information." said Nigel. "No matter how much banner advertising you pay for to try and push the information you want to the top of a search engine or how many lawyers you have that continuously publish injunctions, the information is still there, hidden on page 2 of search results, or hidden within forum comments. It seems that this isn't the first time you have tried to double cross people, and they are not happy about it."

Kimberly, for once, didn't have anything to say. This was the first time someone has stood up to her and she didn't know how to beat them. The silence was eventually broken by one of the suits.

"If there is a recording stating that you have agreed that the copyright belongs to Dave then I am afraid this changes the situation." said the suit with the briefcase. He picked up the contracts from the desk and put them back in the briefcase.

"I would like to make a new offer in the light of recent discussions." the other suit said. "We would like to double your pay and fund your research for a minimum of five years, with the promised foundation, but the understanding that the copyright will be shared between Amstaria and Dave"

Kimberly was now a passenger in the conversation, the lawyers taking over to try and salvage the situation.

Dave however, was suddenly buoyed up by the sudden change in circumstances and by the transformation of Nigel. Dave looked at Nigel and realised the potential that he knew he always had was rising to the surface.

"I would like to make a counter offer" Nigel said without hesitation. "You pay us 12 months salary as severance pay each into our accounts and we walk out of here and we never have to talk to you ever again, with the understanding that I own the parts and Dave owns the copyright to his creation. You can even take the cost price of any parts out of my salary as a matter of goodwill."

Nigel had read all the comments about Kimberly online, but as he had spent many hours reading online, he knew from experience to take things with a pinch of salt. People who felt they have been wronged often go online to vent their frustrations and can exaggerate.

He thought he would give Kimberly a chance to show her true colours. See what she would really do, whether the online comments were the real truth or just exaggerations. He didn't want to end up another helpless victim with his cry for help 10 pages deep in forum comments, but he still had faith in humanity that when push comes to shove, they would do the right thing.

He knew now that this was not a person he wanted to work with and that there was no future here with this company. Even if they offered him what he wanted to hear right now it wouldn't be long before they tried to change the rules once more.

Nigel also had self belief. For once in his life he believed in what Dave and him had accomplished and what they could go on to achieve. It would be easier initially with the backing of a multinational corporation and its vast resources, but he knew they could never achieve what they could on their own. They would always be held back.

Nigel looked over at Dave and Dave stretched out his hand and Nigel shook it. They both turned to Kimberly and the suits with a confident smile on their faces.

The suit with the briefcase turned to face Kimberly and she looked back at him. He didn't speak immediately, he was weighing up the probabilities of each course of action in his head. After a good 10 seconds had passed he finally started speaking, with Kimberly eagerly hoping for a way out of their current situation, some kind of legal loophole that she hadn't thought of, but as soon as the suit started talking she knew it wasn't going to be.

"Kimberly, give them what they want." the suit with the briefcase said.

Kimberly's head fell into her hands. She had lost. For the first time in her career she was beaten. Every meeting in the past she had come out of it feeling invincible, wiping the floor with her adversaries, before walking back to her chauffeur driven car and being driven back to her country estate.

Now she knew what the people on the other side of the table had felt like. It was not a good feeling.

Nigel then got two pieces of folded paper out of his pocket that he had prepared earlier that morning, before placing them on the desk and unfolding them. He smoothed out the folds as best he could and gave one of the copies to Kimberly and the suits, with the other staying their side of the desk.

"Thank you for teaching me to be prepared Kimberly, a very valuable lesson." Nigel said. "This sets out the terms I have asked for, please can you all sign it and then we can be on our way"

"But... but... you can't... there must be something else we can do!" Kimberly begged the suits for a response.

The suit with the briefcase took the paper and read it through.

"I advise you sign this Kimberly. The damage to Amstaria would be devastating if the evidence was released." said the suit with the briefcase.

"That's it is it. We're giving up and letting these two nerds take this from us are we???" Kimberly shouted at the suit, getting properly angry now.

The suit wasn't finished with the bad news yet though.

"The board of directors will not be impressed with this situation when it is communicated what has happened here." The suit finished, before taking a pen and signing Nigel's contract. He handed it over to the other suit who also signed it and then they both signed the other copy of the contract from Nigel's side of the desk.

All that was left now was for Kimberly to counter sign the contract.

"Can't we just keep this between us?" she pleaded with the suits, but they both shook their heads, with one of them handing her the pen, encouraging her to sign the contract.

Reluctantly, she took the pen and signed her signature on both contracts.

One of the suits handed the top copy back to Nigel.

Nigel stood and outstretched his hand over the table to Kimberly. She stood up slowly and then put her hand out and shook Nigel's hand, finally admitting defeat.

Nigel and Dave then stood up and left the office, shutting the door behind them, with the faint sound of sobbing coming from within the closed office.

They walked out of the Amstaria building for the last time into the warmth of sunshine with a feeling of freedom and victory.

Printed in Great Britain
by Amazon

37830744R00076